Zombie

The Cursed Manuscripts

Iain Rob Wright

Ulcerated Press

Dedicated to those who help the helpless.

"Don't judge yourself by what others did to you."
- Cody Kennedy

"A child's first teacher is its mother."
- Peng Liyuan

"The monster never dies."
- Stephen King, *Cujo*

Chapter One

Laura peered out the window, at the trees rushing by in the darkness. The silvery moon seemed to mock her, a faraway destination forever unreachable. If she could only sprout wings, she would take flight and soar above the Earth, spiralling up and up until the air ran out. Anything to not feel like this. To not feel so trapped.

Her breathing was shallow, her head swimming, heart beating fast.

"Will you cheer up, for God's sake?" said Danny, glancing sideways at her. He had both hands clamped around the steering wheel, and he was hunched forward in concentration.

Angry.

And drunk.

I'm angry, too, thought Laura. *Tonight was so humiliating.*

"I'm fine," she said, a petulant mutter. She refused to look at her husband, and didn't particularly wish to speak with him either, as arguing would only make things worse.

It was always better to let things go until moods calmed and tempers eased.

She pinched her thigh and twisted, a distraction from anxiety. And rage.

Danny grumbled. "You're *not* fine, Lor. You're sitting there like a bear with a sore head. It's doing my head in." He switched on the car's high beams as they merged onto an unlit road. As he did so, he clumsily knocked the indicator on and had to cancel the signal with an annoyed grunt. "Fuck's sake."

Laura sighed, knowing he wasn't going to let this go. She could feel him seething in the driver's seat, even without looking at him. "I'm just disappointed that we didn't stay," she admitted. "That's all."

"Oh right," he said. "You're disappointed we didn't stay the night at the family mansion? Excuse me if I'm uncomfortable being surrounded by your dad's wealth. All the poverty and starvation in the world, and some people have kitchens the size of tennis courts. It winds me right up. It's wrong."

Laura rolled her eyes. Danny cared little about poverty whenever they passed a beggar on the street – and he would avoid, like the plague, anyone who tried to approach him with a clipboard. But voicing that out loud, while tempting, wouldn't be worth the blowback. Not while Danny was in such a foul mood.

It was past midnight. Laura's last glass of wine had been over an hour ago, which meant she was sobering up and getting a headache. Despite her grogginess, she couldn't hold her tongue – not when it concerned her parents. "It's not a mansion, Dan. It's a house. A house my dad paid for with his own money and his own hard work. No one ever handed him a thing, so stop acting like success is something to be ashamed of."

"*He* might have worked for it, Lor, but *you* didn't. Why is it fair that I grew up in a flat with broken windows and no carpets while you grew up in a six-bedroom mansion?"

It's not a mansion. Are you trying to cause an argument?

"It's not my fault you had a shitty childhood, Dan. Mine was no picnic either, despite what you like to make out. Either way, they're Rose's grandparents, and she hasn't seen them in eighteen months." She glanced back at their daughter, sleeping in her child's seat with her plump little chin resting against her shoulder. Copper-coloured hair – inherited from Laura – spilled down her face like a silken veil. "I wanted to stay the night," she said. "Is that so wrong? I wanted to spend some time with my mum and dad."

Danny grunted. "Even if it makes me feel like a piece of shit? Christ, you're so selfish, Lor."

I'm *selfish? Are you kidding me?*

She finally turned to look at him, wanting to reach out and strangle him. If only she had the spine to do it. "I don't want to fight with you, Dan. Let's just get home so we can go to bed. Rose will be tired and cranky in the morning, and I'm the one who's going to have to deal with her."

Danny whacked the steering wheel with his palms. "I have work, Lor. What do you want me to say? Do you want me to pay the bills or not?"

She clenched her fists, fingernails digging into her palms. "I'm so tired of this," she said.

"Tired of what?" Danny's anger broke for a moment. A flash of panic crossed his face. "What are you saying, Laura? Tired of what? Me?"

She looked back at Rose again, holding back tears and taking deep breaths to calm the bats flying around in her tummy. "This. Us. The arguing and fighting. I'm tired of you being angry at me all the time."

Danny huffed, but he gave no reply.

The air inside the car grew stuffy as they drove down a straight, undulating road en route to the M5 motorway. It would take them away from Devon and back towards their three-bed semi in Longbridge. With little to no traffic, the journey should take around three hours. By the time they got to sleep, dawn would be depressingly close.

If only we had stayed at my parent's house. We would be having a few last drinks about now, before going upstairs to snuggle up in my nice old bed.

They could have made the long trip home tomorrow, in the brightness of the day, in far kinder moods. She loved Danny to bits – he understood her in ways that no one else did – but sometimes she wanted to kick him right in the face.

Don't be so mean. He tries his best. It's not his fault he's a little messed up.

And he's right about our childhoods. I had everything *as a kid and he had nothing. Being at my parent's house probably did make him feel like shit.*

He just needs to relax and get out of his own head.

I don't want to fight.

Danny rolled his window down halfway and inhaled the rushing air. His messy brown hair fluttered in the breeze, and he squinted, as if the road ahead confused him. How many beers had he downed before bundling her and Rose into their spluttering Nissan Qashqai and speeding off down the driveway? She had begged him not to drive, embarrassed and horrified, but once Danny made his mind up about something, he never changed it.

"I know you wanted to stay," he said, a little less angry,

"but I really *do* have to work, babe. It's bad timing, that's all. We'll drive back down to see your parents soon, I promise."

"How soon?"

"I dunno, do I? Soon. It's only because of lockdowns we haven't seen them more. That's not my fault, is it?"

"Yes, I know Covid isn't your fault, Danny, but Rose needs to see her family." He went to speak, but she cut him off. "*My* family. Not just yours. Mum and Dad want to see their only grandchild."

He nodded, but his expression had turned moody, a subtle shift she knew all too well. A slight narrowing of his eyes, a tautness to his jaw, and inhalations a half-second too long. The national lockdowns during the last eighteen months had brought Danny's grumpy side out on an almost permanent basis. Things were slowly getting better, especially now that he was back at work, but their marriage had not yet fully healed – still punctured and bleeding.

We used to be so happy.

Did we?

Yes. What am I thinking?

Laura didn't want to push Danny too much – it would only drag out his bad mood – so she stayed silent. Eventually, he would calm down and see her point of view, so she would just wait. The problem was that he had utterly humiliated her tonight, and she didn't know whether to scream or cry about it. Her anger was so thick, so viscous, that it made her contemplate leaving him. Once upon a time, that would have seemed absurd. But lately…

I can't imagine myself with anybody else but Dan. Who else would put up with me and all my issues? We just need to work on things. Find a way to stop fighting. Rose deserves a loving home, and I'm not ready to give up on my marriage.

But I can't take any more of this.

Laura leant forward and switched on the Nissan's radio at a low volume. It risked waking Rose, but the tense silence was unbearable. Danny seemed to take it as a hostile act, because he squeezed the steering wheel and put his foot down. The speedometer ticked upwards. He'd been taking things slowly until now, but his anger had clearly dismissed that caution. Thankfully, he slowed down a moment later and sighed.

"Look, I'm really sorry, okay? I know I acted like a twat tonight, but it wasn't on purpose." He shook his head and cleared his throat. "I don't know what's wrong with me sometimes, Lor. You and Rose deserve better, but your dad's house just makes me feel..."

She looked at him. "What?"

"Inadequate. He gave you everything as a kid, but what have *I* given Rose?"

"All the stuff I had growing up doesn't matter, I've told you before. I only ever wanted my mum and dad to spend time with me, but Dad was always working and Mum was... well, she was Mum. Rose loves you, and she gets to be with you every night. That's all she needs. You're a wonderful dad."

His dark expression finally lifted. His sky-blue eyes seemed a little brighter. "I just need to work on being a better husband, huh?"

"Yeah, you do, you dickhead."

With a chuckle, he reached over and squeezed her thigh. She put her hand on top of his and stroked between his knuckles where a thick scar marked a childhood accident. The anger hadn't left her – nowhere near – but she was glad to at least agree on a truce for now. A weight lifted from her chest.

"I'll do better," he said, clearing his throat and refocusing on the road. "I promise."

"I've heard that before."

"I know, but I mean it this time."

"Heard that, too." She chuckled and quickly veered away from the subject. "Hey, you think we can stop and get a McDonald's closer to home? I know me, and I'm gonna be starving."

"Sure. Just like the old days, huh? We'd always grab a Maccies when we were hanging, wouldn't we? Shit, when was the last time we went out together and got proper rat-arsed?"

"Before Rose was born."

He nodded. "Yeah, from the moment you first found out you were pregnant. Wow, that must have been three – four – years ago, then?"

"Must be." She had quit drinking as soon as she'd fallen pregnant with Rose, who was now three years of age. It had indeed been a long time since they'd been rat-arsed together. "Do you miss it?" she asked him.

He was silent for a moment, before shrugging. "I wouldn't change things for the world, but yeah, sometimes I miss it just being us. It used to feel like we were a team, you know? You and me against the world. Partners in crime."

She frowned. "We're still a team. Now more than ever." With a smile, she looked back at their sleeping daughter, then she reached towards the rear-view mirror. She tapped the Mr Bump hanging from it, and the blue and white soft toy swung back and forth, spinning around and dancing. "We're a family now."

Danny nodded, but his smile disappeared. "I suppose you're right. Do *you* ever miss it? Our wild days?"

She thought back to the past, replaying the handful of

years between taking her A levels and beginning a career in HR at the supermarket chain where she now worked. It had been a carefree time of disposable jobs, rapid-fire weekends, and relentless sex. "No," she said. "I don't miss it at all. I enjoyed it at the time, don't get me wrong, and I enjoy looking back on it now, but it's all in the past. Where we are now, that's where I want to be. The present."

Danny chewed the inside of his cheek for a moment, but then he looked at her and grinned. "The present is pretty awesome, huh? I have two wonderful women in my life."

"Yeah, you're a lucky man, so appreciate it."

"Lucky man. Yeah, that's me." He took another deep breath from the air rushing in through his open window. A bitter odour filled the car, perhaps signalling a rainstorm on its way. "I love you, Lor."

"I love you too."

"Love you three times."

"Love you four. Sometimes, I think you forget that."

He sat up straight and cricked his neck, like he was trying to wake himself up. "You're right. I'm an idiot. Okay..." He blew air out of his cheeks. "Let's just move on. The past is a broken glass. Try to fix it and you'll end up cutting yourself."

"That's clever. Did you come up with that yourself?"

"Nah. Peter Schmeichel said it on Match of the Day."

"Well, I'll give you a point for remembering it."

"Thanks."

The tightness in Laura's chest receded as the tension went away. It left her feeling fragile and exhausted. Sometimes, when she and Danny fought, they would refuse to talk to each other for hours – stomping around the house and being dramatic. Other times, they would scream and shout until one of them gave in to tears – usually her. It was easier to get the 'I'm sorrys' and 'I love yous' out of the way quickly and move on. Now, all she needed to do was smooth things over with her parents. She would need to make up an excuse they would believe – that her *dad* would believe – but it wouldn't be easy. Her dad had been all smiles tonight when Danny had hastened them into the car, and he had acted as though he hadn't even noticed Danny's sudden mood shift. But she knew he would use her sudden exit against her at some point when it best suited him. Her dad had a way of making her feel like a scolded child, even at twenty-nine.

I deserve it, though. He's barely seen Rose since she was born, and we just snatched her away in the middle of the night. Mum looked like she was ready to cry. Not that she spoke up and did anything to keep us from leaving.

"I'm sorry you felt uncomfortable at my parent's house." She tried to summon the will to be the bigger person, but it was difficult. "Next time, just talk to me, okay? I'm on your side. I'm always on your side."

Danny appeared embarrassed, which she was used to. Guilt and self-loathing often followed his anger, and he would sometimes grow sullen for days. That could be as bad as the argument itself, so it was worth avoiding.

"I promise," he said. "Next time will be better."

"Okay. Let's just forget it, then. It's over with." She pulled her phone out of her jeans pocket and unlocked the screen. With a throaty sigh, she opened up the messaging app and started typing.

Danny turned his head. "What are you doing?"

"Texting Dad to apologise, and to let him know we're safe. We shouldn't be drink-driving, Dan. It's so irresponsible. We have Rose in the back, and if we—"

Danny shocked her by snatching the phone right out of her hands. He held it away from her, over his shoulder. "Don't you apologise for me. We left because I had work, and that's *it*. End of. I don't need to explain myself to your dad."

"You acted like a dickhead. We were all having a good time, playing cards, and then your mood flipped like it always does. Dad won't believe you got a text from work at eleven o'clock at night. He'll be thinking you made it up as an excuse to leave."

He stared at her, ignoring the road ahead. "You think I'm lying?"

"No, I don't think you're lying. Just let me text my dad, so he knows we're safe, okay? Hey, watch the road, will you?"

He continued glaring at her. "Fuck your dad. Like you said, he wasn't even around when you were growing up. He's a piece of shit. Why don't you see that? Why do you care so much about someone who treats you like dirt? Your mum is like a frightened little mouse."

"Will you just watch the road, Danny? And give me back my phone!"

She tried to grab it, but he tossed it right out of his open window. It disappeared into the darkness, swallowed in an instant.

Laura's mouth fell open. Her eyes went wide. "I... I can't believe you just did that. What the hell, Danny?"

He shrugged like it was nothing – like it was completely normal to throw someone's phone out of a moving vehicle. "You spend too much time on that sodding thing anyway," he said. "Always texting your mates and planning God knows what."

"Are you kidding me?" She shook her head in disbelief.

"What mates? I don't see anybody. I've spent most of the last two years stuck at home with Rose." Her knee bobbed anxiously in the footwell. She pinched her thigh again, trying to keep her temper from bursting forth and making things worse. She couldn't decide if she wanted an ejector seat button or a knife, but she spotted something else instead: Danny's phone. It was sitting in a cradle attached to a heating vent beside the steering wheel. Unable to stop herself, she grabbed it and whipped it across Danny's body, flinging it right out of the window to join whatever fate had befallen hers. "There," she said. "See how you like it."

What the hell did I just do?

My temper. My goddamn temper.

This is going to be bad.

"You psycho!" Danny stamped on the brake and clutch. The tyres squealed, and the Nissan came to a barely controlled stop that threw both of them forward.

Laura cursed and turned in her seat to check on Rose. Her tiny head had rocked back against her chair. Her eyelids flickered, opening briefly, but thankfully she remained asleep.

Danny grabbed Laura's arm and squeezed. "I need my phone for work, you idiot."

"You threw my phone out of the window first!" There was a tremor to her voice, a rising panic mixed with utter incredulity. She still couldn't believe what he had just done. And what she had done in response. They were insane. Both of them.

Danny glared at her, and for the first time, she feared he might lash out and hit her. For almost a full minute, he just sat there, silently glowering. Eventually, he licked his lips and spoke in a weary tone. "All my photos of Rose were on my phone. Damn it."

That hurt, and it made Laura regret what she'd done. Her only defence was that *he* had done it first. "All mine were, too. What the hell did we just do?"

Danny switched off the engine and rubbed at his face with the palms of both hands and then massaged his eyes with his knuckles. After a moment, he yanked up the handbrake and flopped back in his seat. He stared at the beige roof lining ten inches from his nose. "What a night. What a shitty, horrible, awful night."

Laura folded her arms and stared straight ahead at the empty road. Where was the nearest house? Where was the nearest car? It felt so lonely out here in the dark, by themselves, in the middle of the night. "Well, at least we haven't killed each other. Yet."

He groaned. "Why do you always have to make things out to be worse than they are, Lor?"

"To annoy you, obviously."

They sat in silence for a minute, parked in the middle of the road in the middle of the night. It was Danny who spoke first, and he did so as he restarted the engine. "Let's go back a bit and look for my phone. It's probably smashed to pieces, but we might be able to get the photos off it."

Laura offered no words. She just wanted this night to end.

Chapter Two

Danny reversed the Nissan down the road, an unsafe thing to, day *or* night. Laura's stomach was in knots, and she kept glancing back at Rose, anxious that she would wake up. If she started fussing out here, hours away from home, it would be an ordeal sure to make Laura's pounding headache worse.

We could always turn around and go back to Mum and Dad's. Thirty minutes and we could be there.

Danny will say no. Pointless even bringing it up.

Laura could only imagine what her parents were thinking. It had been obvious that Danny had forced her to leave against her wishes, but her mum and dad had just stood there, doing nothing. Did they even care? She supposed they were probably trying to stay out of her marriage – which she was grateful for – yet she felt let down that her dad, at least, hadn't put up a fight to make them stay. He hadn't even mentioned Danny being too drunk to drive.

What could he have done? He was better off saying nothing.

So what exactly am I upset about?

Her parents had witnessed Danny's misbehaviour before – even at their wedding he had been drunk and belligerent – but they never brought it up in front of him. In fact, they only ever gave Laura a hard time. It was *her* fault they didn't visit enough. *Her* fault she and Danny didn't live in a nicer area with better schools for Rose. *Her* failure whenever she asked to borrow money because the bills were higher than expected. Nothing was ever Danny's fault. Even when he was being awful.

Come on, Laura, be fair. He gets anxious and emotional. It's part of why I love him. He's so thoughtful and romantic most of the time. Not to mention he's a great dad to Rose.

Yeah, but sometimes he deserves a big punch in the dick.

She almost laughed at herself, but then remembered the shittiness of the situation. Danny had stopped the car and switched off the engine. The chance of finding their phones was between slim and you've got to be kidding, but at least it would be nice to get some fresh air and calm down a bit. Any more bickering and she might have a full-on panic attack. She'd had several over the last two years.

Just take deep breaths, Lor. Everything's okay. Things'll sort themselves out. They always do.

This is just a bad night.

An awful night.

Laura took off her seatbelt and opened the door, stepping out onto the tarmac. There was nothing on either side of the road except for sinister, shadow-drenched woodland made up of tall, straight trees. The road ahead was like something from a horror movie. With no lampposts or cat's eyes, it stretched only a dozen or so metres before being swallowed up by the darkness beyond the Nissan's headlights. Laura felt like she was standing in a spotlight on an empty planet.

"We should switch on the hazards," she said. "It's not safe being stopped like this."

"Just start looking," said Danny. He crossed the road and stepped onto the grassy verge that led up to the thick line of trees on that side. "There's no one else out here, so stop moaning and help me find my phone."

"All right, fine," she said. "And then you can help me find mine."

Danny grunted.

Laura stepped away from the car, glancing in through the rear window at their sleeping daughter. Tomorrow, she would take Rose to the park to make up for having to leave Nanny and Grandad's early. A bit of time together, on their own, might help Laura clear her head.

Rose deserves better than two parents fighting all the time.

Not wanting to be near Danny for the time being – she needed ten minutes to calm down – Laura crossed the road and kept a few metres back, examining the weeds and kicking at the undergrowth. Danny's mobile was an expensive iPhone, but hers was just a cheap Android. Once upon a time, she had always upgraded to the latest and greatest, but these days she didn't use her phone for much beyond taking pictures of Rose. She and Danny had agreed, years ago, to delete all of their social media accounts. No one wanted their old exes and school bullies getting in contact with them out of the blue, did they? No, they had both agreed that social media was for the vain and shallow. Not for them.

I do miss it occasionally, though.

While the cons outweighed the pros, she had enjoyed keeping up with other people's lives, even from a distance. She had no clue what her old bestie, Liz, was up to these days. They had lost touch right after she and Danny had got married, and shortly before Rose had been born. Adult life had got in the way, and motherhood left little time for friendships.

"I can't believe we're doing this," said Laura, shivering against the cold that was too much for her thin white blouse to repel. The air still had a bitter scent to it, and she was certain that rain was on its way. "We're walking down the side of the road at midnight to find the phones that we ourselves threw out of the window. Seriously, I hate my life."

"It's not our finest moment, I admit it," said Danny, searching ahead, "but it's better to fight than not to, right? Just means we're passionate."

"Some might say mental."

He stopped and turned back. "Well, who wants to be normal?"

Laura stopped as well, wanting to maintain the distance. "I do, Danny! I want to be normal and happy and not arguing all the time."

"Then stop arguing. This is funny if you think about it."

"I don't feel like laughing. I feel like crying."

He put his hands on his hips and groaned. "Come on, don't be like that, babe. It was only a fight. We always get over them. It's just been a tough couple of years, with the lockdowns and stuff. We're just a little fed up with each other."

She kicked at the weeds and examined the shadows. "I'm just upset. And tired. Can we get back in the car, please? It's cold, and I think it's starting to rain."

He put his hands out to his sides. "I don't feel anything."

"All the same. We're not going to find our phones, so

let's just go. I need to be up with Rose in the morning, and you have work."

Unexpectedly on a Sunday. Yeah, right.

Danny nodded. "Ten minutes. Ten minutes and we'll get going, all right? I really don't want to lose all those pictures of Rose. Do you?"

Laura sighed. While they had backed up most of their pictures on their home computer, there would still be one or two they hadn't got around to yet. It was worth taking another ten minutes to look, she supposed. "Fine."

She kicked at the grass again, wishing for Danny's phone to just suddenly materialise so they could move on to finding hers and then get back in the car. Her foot struck rocks here and there, giving her false hope, but there was no sign of what she was looking for. The phone could be lying in the grass three feet away from her and she wouldn't know it.

And I'm freezing my tits off.

She shivered and clutched at herself, considered grabbing her coat from the boot, but hoped to be gone by the time the need grew too great. Staring off into the trees, she once again felt like she was in a horror movie, and her mind conjured axe-wielding maniacs and werewolves. She dispelled the absurd images with a chuckle. The real monsters of the world were more mundane.

Like moody husbands.

Despite not believing in monsters, Laura still flinched at the sound of a twig snapping. Her breath caught in her chest, and she instinctively glanced back towards their car on the other side of the road. It was about twenty feet away behind her, and she couldn't see Rose inside because the interior lights had switched off. Once again her mind taunted her, creating scenarios of returning to the car to find Rose missing.

Screw the phones. We'll buy new ones.

I really want to get out of here.

Another branch snapped, causing Laura to watch the shadowy gaps between the tall trees. Something moved nearby, a grey shape in the darkness, and something glinted. Eyes. She blinked and rubbed at her face, hoping she was seeing things, but when she looked again, the grey blob was even closer. It took on the form of a creature.

Laura's bladder suddenly demanded release.

The creature moved in her direction.

She went to scream, forgetting her fight with Danny and now wanting him right beside her, but before she could make a sound, the creature broke free of the shadows and caused her to freeze.

What the...?

The fox was larger than she thought foxes ought to be, and while it had slender, concave flanks, its back and chest were square and solid – powerful. The animal studied Laura, its twitching ears pinned forward. A bushy tail wafted back and forth lazily behind it. It made no sound.

Neither did Laura.

Danny must have sensed the silence, because he turned back. He gasped as he noticed the fox, and then he slowly looked over at Laura. Laura did everything she could to beg him with her expression. *Please. Help.*

Danny moved, rushing towards Laura and shooing the fox away. "Get out of here!" he yelled. "Go on, get!" He waved his arms over his head and hissed. The fox, not the least bit concerned, turned casually and slunk back into the trees. It made an odd *yipping* sound and then was gone.

Danny reached for Laura and threw his arms around her. "You okay?"

"Yeah, I'm fine. It was just a fox. Wasn't expecting it, that's all."

"It was a big 'un, huh?" He was panting slightly, as rattled as she was, but he was smiling too with relief. "What an absolute unit."

"Did you know they could get that big?"

He shrugged. "I grew up on a council estate in Selly Oak. What do I know about foxes?"

"Good point. Can we just get out of here, please?" She looked back towards the car, which suddenly seemed so far away. "If Rose wakes up, she'll be scared."

Danny exhaled through his nose and nodded. "Yeah, okay. A couple of phones aren't worth getting eaten alive by foxes for."

She punched him on the arm and laughed. "Foxes don't eat people. I'm embarrassed for even being scared."

"Reminds me of the time that sparrow got into our old flat. You screamed the entire building down." He leapt backwards into the road, hands above his head, doing an impression of her wailing in panic. "It's in my hair. It's in my hair."

She put a finger to her lips and tried to shush him, but she couldn't help chuckling. "Be quiet. You'll wake Rose."

He stopped flapping about and grew serious. "Okay. Okay, I'm sorry. Can we just make up? It's been a rough couple of hours and I really need a cuddle."

A cuddle sounded good, but she was still angry and upset. "Tonight was horrible, Dan. I don't understand why these things keep happening. It's like, as soon as I let myself go and start to have a good time, you get angry."

"I don't get angry."

"Then what? What happened tonight, Dan? Why couldn't you just relax and have fun? It's not normal."

"Oh, so I'm not normal now?"

She looked down at the ground and bit her tongue. *Maybe I should say it. Maybe I should tell him I've been thinking of leaving. No, if I say it, I won't be able to take it back, and breaking up isn't what I want.* "I love you, Dan, but sometimes you make life really hard. You cause issues where there doesn't need to be any. And you don't trust me, which isn't fair. I don't know what to do any more. I don't know how to help you."

For a moment, he didn't reply. There was the possibility of him getting angry and defensive, but for now, he remained calm. He took a deep breath and let it out through his nostrils. "Something just comes over me, Lor. I try to relax, to be happy in the moment, but..."

"But what?"

"I don't know. Like I said, something just comes over me. There's this voice in the back of my head that takes over. Maybe I need to see a doctor."

She shrugged. "Maybe. What harm could it do?"

"None, I guess. It's not just me, though." His calmness faltered and his expression turned a little moodier. He folded his arms. "You can be a real bitch when you want to be, Lor. I get back from work some days and all you do is give me grief. You push me, prod me, until I have no choice but to lose my temper."

She didn't want things to escalate, so she tried to meet him halfway. "I know I'm not perfect, Dan. I can see a doctor as well. Whatever it takes for us to be happy."

"I thought we *were* happy?"

"Most of the time. Not always."

His defensiveness went away, and he seemed to deflate. "We'll make a plan. Let's just get home first."

"Sounds good."

"I'd still like a cuddle, though. Come here, ginge."

"Don't call me that, you git." She exhaled, torn between anger and affection. After a moment, she stepped forward to join him in the middle of the road. "You're lucky I'm so forgiving. If I wasn't, then—"

Headlights lit up the darkness as a vehicle sped towards them.

Laura's voice caught in her throat.

Danny half turned and put his hands up, but he didn't step out of the road. He didn't step out of the way.

He's going to get run over.

The approaching vehicle veered onto the wrong side of the road to avoid the parked Nissan twenty metres ahead of it. It was now headed right towards Danny. The driver blared his horn.

Laura lunged and grabbed Danny by the sleeve of his jumper, yanking him sideways onto the grass. He tripped over his own feet and the two of them went sprawling just as the van hurtled past.

The driver slammed on the brakes.

Tyres squealed.

The horn blared endlessly.

Laura landed on her hip and looked desperately towards the road. The van's headlights arced away from her as the vehicle careened back into the correct lane.

Now speeding right towards the parked Nissan.

Laura screamed. "Rose!"

But it was too late.

Chapter Three

The van collided with the Nissan, making a sound so violent that Laura couldn't help but close her eyes and cover her ears. When she looked again, the van was on its side, skidding along the road and sending up sparks, while the Nissan rocked on its springs, shunted off the road and onto the grassy verge.

Laura realised she was screaming at the top of her lungs. Danny was doing the same.

Rose. Rose was asleep in the car.

Oh God. Oh God.

Laura clambered to her feet and sprinted across the road, crying out for her baby. When she heard Rose's terrified whimpers, it was the worst thing she'd ever heard in her life. It was also the best.

She's alive. My baby's alive.

By this time, Danny was on his feet as well, racing across the road behind her. Usually, he would have been the quicker of the two, but the fireworks exploding inside Laura made her move faster than her body would usually allow. Their car had slid half off the road, its front tyres digging two deep trenches in the grass. Its headlights shone off into the nearby woods, illuminating the trees and giving them back their colour. Around twenty feet away, the upturned van lit up the empty road ahead.

"Rose!" Laura reached the car. "Rose, it's okay."

"Mummy!" Her daughter's pitiful cries were heartrending.

Laura snatched frantically at the door handle.

But the door gave only a single inch before sticking. It was jammed.

"Rose!"

Laura felt woozy. She had to steady herself against the car, but its clean curves and angles had become distorted and jagged. Maroon paint had come away in slashed ribbons, and a cracked headlight hung by a tangle of wires. The largest dent was behind the front wheel arch on the driver's side.

Laura yanked on the rear door handle repeatedly, growing ever more hysterical as it refused to budge. "It won't open. It won't open!"

"Here!" said Danny in a high-pitched voice. He moved Laura aside and grabbed the door handle for himself, while offering soothing words to Rose inside. The anxious quiver in his voice was not reassuring, but Laura could only stand back helplessly. Despite the adrenaline in her system, Danny was still much stronger than her. Trying to stay calm, she glanced down the road towards the van. It had bounced off the front of the Nissan and flipped onto its side before sliding along in a shower or sparks. One of its rear panel doors had sprung open to reveal a rectangle of darkness inside. Was the driver okay? He wasn't making any noise.

"Got it!" Danny yanked the crumpled rear door open

with a relieved grunt. It opened awkwardly, angled towards the floor, but at least it opened.

The interior lights flicked on. Danny had switched off the engine, but not the ignition. Rose was still strapped in her car seat, screaming and yelling. When she saw Danny, she reached out with both hands while he unbuckled her and snatched her up into his powerful arms. "It's okay, rose-bud," he soothed. "Daddy's got you. Daddy's here. Shh-shh-shh."

While Danny held Rose, Laura checked her over, lifting her frizzy red hair away from her forehead and checking for cuts. She rubbed at her daughter's chubby little arms and legs, checking for lumps and breaks. Everything appeared – and felt – normal.

Thank God.

"Tell me if it hurts, baby, okay?" Laura continued, checking for injuries as Rose buried her head in Danny's neck. She wasn't acting hurt, just scared. Who could blame her?

"I'm getting her off the road," said Danny. "What do we do, Lor? We can't even call for help."

Because we tossed our phones out of the window like a pair of nutters.

Laura covered her face and moaned. "This is a night-mare. Please, just tell me I'm dreaming."

Danny closed his eyes for a second. His face was ashen, and his Adam's apple bobbed up and down. "There's some-thing else to think about," he said. "I drank six beers before we left. If the police breathalyse me, I've had it. I'll lose my licence. Or worse."

"Christ, this just keeps getting worse and worse." She looked back towards the van, wanting to scream but feeling more likely to pass out. Her legs were vibrating twigs, ill-equipped to take her weight.

Get it together, Lor.

Rose was okay, and that was the main thing, but it meant they now needed to take a breath and deal with things sensibly. Other people were involved in this. "We need to check on the driver," she said. "He hasn't come out yet. He could be trapped."

"You're right. Do you want to hold Rose?"

She nodded and reached out for her daughter. "Okay, baby-girl. Come to Mummy."

Rose was trembling, so Laura squeezed her tightly and stepped off the road with her. When she saw the damage to the Nissan from another angle, she hissed. If they had just put the hazard lights on, like she had suggested, this might never have happened.

We're to blame for this. Parked in the middle of the road at night. The driver probably never even saw our car until it was too late. Even then, he swerved to avoid it.

Then he had to swerve right back again to avoid killing Danny. There was nothing he could do.

This is going to end badly. Hell, it started *badly.*

If Danny lost his plumbing job due to not having a driving licence they would struggle to pay the bills. Laura only worked two days a week – while Rose was at nursery – and they couldn't survive on a single part-time wage. If the van's driver was badly injured, things could be even worse. Danny might go to prison.

That's crazy. No one is going to prison.

Are you sure about that, Lor?

We could lose Rose.

Her mind taunted her once again, creating images of Danny finding the van driver dead, bundling them into the car, and fleeing the scene. They would make it home, but only to wait anxiously for the knock at the door that would bring the police.

Laura had to fight the urge to keel over and vomit.

Don't assume the worst. Not yet. Wait for Danny to check things out first.

Danny crept towards the upturned van, glancing back periodically as if he feared another vehicle might appear out of the darkness and add even more fuel to this quickly spreading fire. Holding Rose with one arm, Laura checked her leather and gold watch. It had just turned 1am, but it felt like several hours had passed since they'd left her parent's house. What would things look like another hour from now? Better?

Or worse?

"Hey!" Danny called out. "Are you okay? Can you answer me?"

No answer.

Danny glanced back at Laura, a grim expression on his face. What should they do if they found the driver in bad shape? How would they call for help? *Should* they call for help?

Of course we should. What other option is there?

We run. Pretend this never happened and hope for the best.

No.

"Stay back."

Danny flinched. Laura did too. The driver was alive.

Thank God.

"It's okay," said Danny, yelling towards the van. "You've been in an accident, but we're going to get you help, okay? What's your name?"

"Back. You need... to stay back."

Danny picked up his pace and hurried to the front of the van. He tiptoed to look inside through the broken side window that now faced the sky. "Shit," he said. "All right, mate. You're going to be fine, okay? Let's just get you out of there." He reached an arm in through the broken window. "Easy does it."

Laura rocked Rose in her arms, kissing the top of her head. Then she called out. "Is he okay, Danny? What are you doing?" Rose flinched in her arms, so she shushed her. "Tell me what's happening."

"He's stuck inside, Lor. But I think... I think he's okay."

Laura tossed back her head and sighed with relief. *Thank God, no one's dead.*

Danny reached into the van and started pulling, but the driver protested. He kept telling Danny to get away from him, sounding hysterical, probably in shock.

"Come on, mate. Help me out here. There might be another car along any minute. It's safer outside. Damn it, stop fighting me." Danny had always been deceptively strong – only five nine, but he had spent his youth playing rugby – yet, even at a distance, Laura could see the sinews bulging in his neck as he fought desperately to hoist the unseen driver upwards.

Laura shushed Rose again, and kept rocking her back and forth, but she kept her eyes on the scene ahead. Why was the driver so reluctant to be helped? Was he in shock? Pain?

He must be.

"Okay, mate," said Danny, finally yanking the driver up through the broken window. "I've got you. Just hold on to me. That's it." He wrapped his arms around the driver – middle-aged and stained with blood – and yanked him free of the van, but when he tried to set the man down on the road, he immediately collapsed. It was as if his legs couldn't support his weight. He groaned in agony and beat his fists against Danny's thigh, causing Laura to wonder if he was angry about their recklessness that had caused the crash. If so, there went any chance of them claiming innocence.

Danny hopped out of harm's way as the van driver continued punching at him. "Easy there, mate. Let's just get you off the road, okay? Hey, fucking stop that."

Laura took a step deeper into the long grass, wanting to be away from the road. Something felt wrong here. The driver was acting weird; not angry, like she had first thought, but more like he was worried. Or afraid. He shoved and punched at Danny from the ground, ordering him away. "Get the hell out of here. You don't want to be here."

Danny clearly didn't understand. He knelt to grab the driver, who tried to fight him off, but Danny was the stronger of the two – and uninjured – so he won the battle easily. Clutching the driver beneath the arms, he dragged the man along the ground towards the rear of the van.

Laura spotted movement in the van's rear compartment, and her ears detected a scrabbling sound, like something brushing up against the metal panels inside. An animal, perhaps? Had a dog been in the back of the van when it had crashed?

Wouldn't a dog be whining or barking?

"Danny?" Laura waved an arm. "Come back. Something doesn't feel right."

Danny glanced over his shoulder and frowned at her. The driver was still trying to fight him off. "What are you talking about?"

"There's something in the back of the van. There's something moving about in there."

The driver groaned. "Y-You idiots. Get away from me. Put me down. Go!"

Danny shook his head, confused. He propped the driver up against the van's roof – now vertical – and finally lost his temper. "What the hell is wrong with you, man? I'm tryna help you."

"You've fucked us!" As the driver sat up, his arms and chest bulged, revealing him to be a well-built, tough-looking man. He wore desert boots and dark blue overalls. As his strength returned, his voice grew more forceful. "Damn it. I need to call this in. You... You goddamn morons."

Danny was clearly at a loss. "Call *what* in? Just calm down and tell me what's wrong."

The driver moaned, patting himself down, still slightly dazed, but growing more and more alert. "Just shut up, will you? I need to deal with this."

"You've lost the plot, mate."

Laura called out, realising she had involuntarily crept closer to the road. "Dan, please. Come back."

Something emerged from the darkness inside the rear of the van. A pale, almost ghostly hand clasped the edge of the opening. Someone was back there.

A passenger? A prisoner?

What the hell is going on?

"Danny! There's someone else here. Be careful."

Be careful of what? Why am I so afraid?

I need to protect Rose.

From what?

Danny hurried to the back of the van, arriving just in time to see a face emerge from the shadowy interior. It belonged to a man, grotesque and ugly. Wispy black strands of hair hung from his head, but he was mostly bald. Gaps in his mouth betrayed missing teeth.

"Danny, get back here now. Please, just come to me."

Danny hopped away from the van, back-pedalling towards Laura and Rose. He seemed to, at last, realise that something was wrong. His instincts kicked in and he started backing away.

Rose's face was pressed against Laura's shoulder, which she was glad for, because she didn't want her three-year-old daughter to see whatever... whatever *this* was.

Who is that man? Why was he in the back of the van?

What's wrong with him?

Danny reached Laura at the side of the road, half out of breath. He put both hands on his head and gasped. "What the hell is wrong with that guy? He looks sick. Real sick."

A lump of revulsion trapped itself in Laura's throat and filled her mouth with saliva. "I don't like this, Dan. This isn't right."

Still slumped against the van, the driver looked over and shouted, "Get in your car and go. You were never here, okay?" He produced a chunky, old-fashioned phone from a pouch on his belt and started tapping at the keypad frantically.

"He's calling for help," said Danny.

"He said we should leave."

"We can't do that. He's hurt."

The driver glared back at them again. "Go, you fools! Leave!"

Attracted by the man's shouting, the sickly figure emerged fully from the back of the van, dressed in dirty clothes too big for him. He sniffed at the air, a strange, animalistic gesture. The driver was mumbling to himself as he fiddled with his phone, and it caused the grotesque man to stagger around the corner to investigate. When the driver saw him, he panicked. "Shit! You got out? Fuck-fuck-fuck."

He tried to get up, but his legs once again failed him. He dragged himself along like a slug instead, leaving a dark trail on the road behind him. Something below his knee glistened, a bone broken free of the flesh. He wasn't going to get away. No chance in hell.

"I need to help him," said Danny, taking a half step forward.

Laura grabbed him by the arm. "Don't you dare. Stay here with me and Rose."

"But he's hurt. He needs our help. That other guy must be an escaped prisoner or something."

Laura didn't know what was happening, but she felt it vital that Danny did not go back to help. This was no escaped prisoner. "You've been drinking," she said. "The last thing we need is any more trouble. Let's just get in the car and leave. He wanted us to leave."

Am I really that cold? Am I prepared to leave an injured man who needs our help?

I don't know what's going on and I'm fucking terrified.

So, yes, I'm prepared to leave.

The grotesque man fell on top of the driver, like he was playing rugby and wanted to keep the other man down. The driver screamed; at first, screams of fear, but then screams of agony. A sickening sound followed, wet and meaty.

Laura's mouth fell open. She squeezed Rose tightly against her chest.

"Too tight, Mummy."

Danny gasped. "He's... He's..."

Laura finished the sentence for him. "He's *eating* him."

"Too tight, Mummy."

Laura eased up on her daughter. "S-Sorry, sweetheart." She turned to Danny. "We have to get out of here. Right now!"

"Help me." The driver screamed at them in a gurgle, no longer ordering them away. Now, he was just a desperate man begging for help. "Please..."

Rose trembled in Laura's arms – too many wild screams and too much panicked shouting for a three-year-old to process – and she began to sob. Laura shushed her, but she, too, panicked when she saw Danny take off towards the van. "Danny, no!"

"I have to help him."

"Mummy, I want to go home. I'm cold. It's loud."

Laura was torn between chasing after Danny and keeping Rose safe, but the latter easily won out. "It's okay, sweetheart," she said. "We'll be home soon."

Home is three hours away – and we smashed up our car.

What the hell are we going to do?

Danny grabbed the cannibalistic maniac from behind, wrapping an arm around his throat and hurling him to the ground, where he landed awkwardly. There was the resounding snap of a breaking bone, yet he didn't cry out in pain.

Danny went to help the driver, who was now jabbering hysterically, blood spurting from his mouth and creating a fine mist in the glow of the van's rear lights. "M-M-My phone. Y-Y-You need to call the number."

"What number?" Danny bent at the knees but didn't dare touch the bloody man. "What number?"

"The... The only one. Call it. Now."

Danny searched the ground for the driver's phone and spotted it lying a few feet away. He reached down to grab it, but the maniac grabbed him first, seizing his wrist and yanking him off balance. He tripped over his own feet, one arm twisting behind him, and then he fell.

Laura stifled a scream as she saw – and heard – her

husband's skull crack against the road, but she was relieved when she saw him fight back immediately as his attacker fell on top of him. He landed a fierce blow from underneath, thumping the maniac in his chin, but when he tried to grab the man by the throat, he missed and grabbed thin air.

The maniac dropped his head and bit down on Danny's wrist, causing him to cry out in pain. The agony must have galvanised him, because an animalistic growl escaped his lips, and he heaved his attacker away in a fit of punches and kicks. Like a pit bull, the other man tried to keep a bite hold on his wrist, but his jaws eventually opened up and he was forced to let go.

Danny wasted no time getting back to his feet.

His attacker attempted to get up after him, but he struggled, one arm dangling limply by his side and snapped backwards at the elbow. He managed to make it up onto his knees, but Danny viciously booted him in the side of the head and sent him crashing against the upturned roof of the van.

The man collapsed to the road and went still.

And then immediately rose again.

Laura gasped. Danny had just kicked the man's skull like a football, but he didn't even seem to have felt it. Was he on drugs? Cocaine?

"G-Get your little girl out of here," the driver moaned, choking on his own blood. "Before it's too late."

Danny appeared to have frozen, and it wasn't until Rose began wailing that he broke free from the shock and hurried back towards Laura. When he reached her, he was clutching his wrist and hissing in pain. "The bastard bit me. He's insane."

"He's coming," said Laura, and it was true. The maniac had made it back to his feet and was now stumbling rapidly towards them like a belligerent drunk. "Danny, what do we do?"

Danny was out of breath and clearly hurt. It was impossible to inspect his wound because he held his wrist flat against his stomach, but blood was gushing down the front of his jumper. "The car," he said to her weakly. "Get back inside the car."

Laura nodded and hurried over to the Nissan. She yanked open the back door while carrying Rose one-handed and shuffled across the rear seats. Dumping her daughter – a little too harshly – into her child seat, she then turned and slammed the door closed. Meanwhile, Danny headed around to the driver's side and reached for the handle. Before he made it in, the maniac arrived and grabbed him around the neck. Leaning in with broken teeth, he tried to bite Danny's throat, but Danny held him at bay with one arm while half turning and trying to open the driver's door behind him. He managed to open it an inch before his attacker crushed him against the side of the car, their full weight bearing down. The man snapped his jaws at Danny, trying to clamp down on flesh. Danny's wounded wrist smeared blood all over the car's side window as he struggled to keep on his feet.

"Fuck off!" he yelled. "Just fuck right off!" He shoved the maniac away with both hands and bought himself a few feet of space, allowing him enough time to open the door and slide inside the car. Before the maniac could attack again, he slammed the door closed and held it.

It was like closing the lid on Pandora's box. Suddenly, the maddening chaos – the shouting and the moaning – became muffled.

Rose wailed in the back seat.

Laura sobbed. Her head pounded, and she wanted to throw up.

Danny reached forward and engaged the door locks, then flopped back in his seat, panting and moaning and using every swear word he could think of. Meanwhile, a violent man, as ugly as a corpse, beat at the windows, trying to get in.

Chapter Four

"Drive away," Laura urged. "Hurry."

The key was still in the ignition, so Danny twisted it. The dashboard came to life, instrument panels adding light to the darkness. A *tick-tick-tick* accompanied the glow, but there was no reassuring grumble of an engine. Danny rotated the key again and again, but the Nissan wouldn't start. He punched the steering wheel and growled. "We're not going anywhere."

Laura was trembling. No – more than that – her entire body was *quaking*. How had this night gone so utterly, unbelievably wrong? Had they crashed on the highway and gone to Hell?

I let Danny drive drunk.

With Rose in the back.

The maniac rapped at their windows, slithering along the side of the car and trying to find a way in. Rose saw him and hid her face, squealing in fright. Danny sat up front in silence, rubbing at his forehead and blinking. Laura was no expert, but she feared he was going into shock. His wrist was bleeding all over his lap. "Dan? Dan, do we need to take care of your arm?"

"Huh?"

"Your arm." She leant forward between the front seats and nodded at his wound. "We need to stop it from bleeding."

"It's fine."

"It's not fine. Come on, let's take a look at—"

They both flinched as the maniac crashed against the driver's side window. His mouth hit the glass and his lips burst open, oozing a murky brown fluid. The man's eyes were the colour of spoilt milk.

"He's mindless," said Laura, staring out of the window and trying to make sense of what she was seeing. "What's wrong with him? Is it drugs?"

Danny huffed, and he seemed to snap back to reality, turning to study the man at the window. "You and I took our fair share of drugs as teenagers, Lor. You ever hear of anything that can do this to a man? He's diseased... cancer or something. Or what's that old thing people used to get where their flesh rotted away?"

"Um..." The word came to her unexpectedly from the back of her brain. "Leprosy? You think he has leprosy?"

"I don't know. Maybe the van driver was taking him somewhere for treatment – a hospital, maybe. Or a secret fucking lab."

Laura pictured men in bright yellow spacesuits carrying test tubes full of infectious diseases. Lying on beds in the background, inside see-through tents, she saw herself and Danny covered in bulbous blisters and lesions. Dying.

What have we been exposed to?

Outside on the road, the van driver, still alive, let out a pitiful moan. Laura peered through the windscreen and watched as he crawled along the road. Once again, his rambling attracted the maniac, who turned away from the Nissan and headed back towards the van.

"Shit," said Danny. "He's going back to finish what he started."

"Don't even think about going out there," said Laura. "You're hurt."

Danny glanced down at his wrist and nodded. "It would be too late, anyway. He's bleeding from a dozen places. That nutcase dug into him like a kebab."

Laura didn't know what to say to that, so she focused on something else, putting her hands on Rose and rubbing her arms. She'd caught a chill, so Laura kept rubbing until she warmed up. "Are you okay, honey?"

Rose had tears in her eyes. "Want Grandad."

"We'll see him soon, I promise."

"Nasty man," she said, looking out the window.

Laura nodded, and once again she didn't know what to say.

Danny hissed from up front. "Shit, Lor, my wrist is killing me." He held it up to reveal a glistening wound in the shape of two jagged crescents. The bottom crescent had a deep puncture in it, and that was where all the blood was coming from.

"Can you tear off your sleeve?" he asked her.

"My sleeve?"

"Yeah, to wrap my wrist up. I have to stop it bleeding like this."

Laura understood his intention. He was wearing a striped blue woollen jumper with D&G across the front, and it was far too thick to tear apart. Laura, however, was wearing a long-sleeved blouse that would be far easier to rip into strips. So she tried, tugging at the seam across her shoulder. At first, the threads tore easily, but then they reached a certain point and refused to rip any more. "I can't... I can't get it."

Danny grunted impatiently. "Come here. Lean over." He snatched at her sleeve – also pinching the skin at the back of her arm – and then gave it a hard yank. It forced Laura forward against the seats and made her yelp in surprise. Instead of apologising, he yanked again, and then again, until the sleeve tore loose with a satisfying *riiiip*. He then offered the fabric back to her. "I can't tie it one-handed."

Feeling battered, Laura took the sleeve and began wrapping it around Danny's wrist, pulling it tight, and then grimacing as it turned dark with blood. A coppery stench filled the car.

"How's that?" she asked once she was done.

"Better. Thanks."

Outside, the driver howled as the maniac fell upon him again. It only took a moment for him to fall silent for good.

"We should run while he's busy eating," said Danny.

Laura shook her head. "What about Rose?"

"I'll carry her."

"With one arm? What if you get tired and have to stop? You're white as a sheet. I'm not even sure you *can walk, let alone* run."

Danny let out a breath and slumped in his seat. "You're right. I feel like I'm about to pass out. I don't know what to do, Lor. How do we get ourselves out of... whatever this is?"

"We stay inside the car." She stared out the window at the feasting maniac, adamant that trying to leave would be the worst idea ever. What could cause a man to eat living human flesh? What level of psychosis would have to take hold? Working in HR, Laura had plenty of experience dealing with various mental issues – although typically mild – but she had never heard of anything that could turn a man into a ghoul. The thought of going back outside, with that thing hunting them...

I can't do it. I can't go out there. Not unless Danny can protect me.

"We stay here and wait for help," she said, trying to reassure the both of them. "The doors are locked and we're warm. Someone will have to drive past eventually and call for help."

Danny shook his head, as if he were unconvinced. His eyelids appeared heavy. "And then what? They get out to investigate, only to be eaten by that psychopath? That's if he doesn't smash our windows in first. We're sitting ducks."

Laura leant back against the seat and resumed rubbing Rose's upper arms to soothe her. If she and Danny behaved calmly, their daughter might settle. "He didn't even try the handles to get in," she said as she replayed the scene in her mind. "He didn't speak, or show any emotion at all. It's like he's an animal."

"What kind of animal doesn't feel pain, Lor? I heard his arm snap, and he didn't even make a peep."

Laura searched to see the maniac's current location. He was still hunched over the dead van driver, chewing away hungrily. His left arm was snapped backwards at the elbow, which must have been an agonising injury, yet he did nothing to acknowledge it. The limb just dangled by his side.

"Are you okay?" asked Danny, suddenly focused and alert, like he had just been jolted awake. "Are you or Rose hurt?"

Laura shook her head. They were both fine, besides being terrified. Rose had her face buried against the side of her chair, and she was fidgeting sleepily. It was approaching 2am in the morning. How much traffic would come this way so late at night? Surely no road in the South remained deserted, even in the small hours? Somebody would head past eventually.

But when?

How long are we going to be trapped in here?

"I'm sorry about tonight," said Danny. "This is all my fault."

Laura chuckled, but it was humourless. "Yep. We could be in a nice, warm bed right now. I think I actually hate you."

"I hate me a bit, too." He turned and put a hand against her cheek. It was clammy with blood. "We're going to get out of this, Lor. Just let me catch my breath and then I'll figure something out. I'll keep us safe. We'll... We'll..." He shuddered, almost convulsing. "We'll make a run for it. Soon."

"Are you okay, Danny?"

"Just need a minute."

He was in no shape to run right now, and she was glad of it. To her, it still felt much safer to stay inside the car. What if they made a break for it, only to trip while carrying Rose? Or what if the maniac outside was faster than they thought? There were too many unknowns.

Danny was shivering, so Laura reached forward and tried to turn on the heating, but with the engine off it did nothing. Thankfully, it was early October and not the middle of December. They probably wouldn't freeze out here by the side of the road like a pensioner without a blanket.

That's horrible. What am I thinking?

I'm losing it.

The maniac finally finished his meal and stood up, leaving the van driver's body in tatters. Instead of heading back towards the Nissan, he wandered into the middle of the road and started stumbling around in circles.

"He's forgotten about us," said Laura, feeling a twinge of hope as she realised it to be true. "It's like he doesn't even remember we're in here."

Danny nodded, blinking slowly. "You're... You're right."

"Maybe, if we stay quiet and keep still, he'll go away."

It was as good a plan as any they had, so the two of them shifted down in their seats and made themselves less visible. Rose was tumbling back towards slumber, breathing deeply and flinching every few seconds. Outside, the maniac continued to shuffle back and forth, seeking no destination. It really was as if he were braindead.

Or just plain dead.

Bile leapt into Laura's throat, and she had to force it back down as the grim thought taunted her again.

Dead.

She peered over the dashboard, studying the shambling figure outside. Then she examined the streaks of chunky pus that the maniac had left on the outside of the window. No human being could be in such a poor state and still be on their feet. Could they?

He isn't rotting away from leprosy or some other horrible disease. He's a corpse, risen from the dead. A zombie.

Ha!

"Dan, I think—"

Danny shushed her before she could voice her concerns. "Hold on," he said. "Something's happening."

"What?" She looked out of the window, angling her head back and forth. "What's happening?"

"The van driver. Look! He's moving."

Laura pushed herself into the gap between the front seats and looked out of Danny's side window, which offered the best view of the road. The van driver was indeed moving, one leg twitching like he was receiving an electric shock. Was it what they called a death rattle? The last signals clearing out of the brain, like a computer powering down?

Danny shook his head, eyes bugging out of his head. His complexion appeared grey in the dim glow coming from the dashboard. "How can he still be alive?"

"He can't be," said Laura, worrying that she was about to get confirmation of her burgeoning – and absurd – theory. "He can't be alive."

The driver sprang up into a sitting position, as if his upper half had just been yanked by invisible ropes. He glanced around vacantly, like a newborn calf, and then clambered to his feet. On his broken leg, he shuffled over to join his murderer in the centre of the road. There, the two of them commenced a merry dance, stumbling around and around.

Danny continued to shake his head. "I-I don't understand. How is he back on his feet?"

Laura tried to blink, but she couldn't look away, not even for a second. "Zombies," she said. "They're zombies."

Danny looked at her like she was mad, but he didn't argue.

Chapter Five

"What are you talking about, Lor?"

"They're dead, Danny. You kicked that man right in the skull, and he got right back to his feet. He broke his arm and didn't even flinch. And what about the driver? You watched him being torn apart, but now he's up and about like he's ready for round two."

"He's in shock."

"He's dead, Danny. Just look at him."

Danny looked out of his window. The Nissan was now at an angle, facing more towards the trees than the road, and its bonnet was angled down into a dip. The dangling right headlight cast light onto only a narrow section of the road, but the van's rear lamps created another small cone of light nearby, which the two dead men stumbled in and out of, dipping in and out of the shadows. They shambled around like you would expect walking corpses to, and their flesh hung, twisted and torn, from their bones. The van driver leaked blood from a dozen places, but the other man not at all. Instead, he shed chunks of skin and flesh, peppering the road with gore.

"They're dead, Dan. Or infected with something more terrible than we can understand. We need to get out of here."

Danny said nothing. His head slumped to the side, like he had grown too weak to hold it up any longer. Laura had to grab his shoulder to regain his attention. "Are you okay?"

He put a hand over his bandaged wrist and winced. "Yeah. I'm just trying to breathe through the pain. I feel sick. Dizzy."

Laura nodded. She wished she could tell him to lie back and close his eyes, but she needed him alert. She needed him to get them out of this somehow. Her hands trembled in her lap. "Danny, I'm terrified."

He turned to look at her, his pupils large and unfocused. "It's okay," he said. "Just give me a minute and I'll clear up the mess. I'll clear it all up. The mess."

With dismay, Laura realised he was falling asleep. She shook him again by the shoulder, but he didn't respond. When he had spoken, he had done so dreamily, and the words he had used took Laura back in time.

The mess.

She had met Danny seven years ago when she had been a fresh-faced twenty-two-year-old living away from home. Yet to settle into a career in HR, she had been working part-time at a brand-name clothing store on Solihull high street while studying at Birmingham City University to be a nurse. During her lunch break, she would often get a coffee from the greasy spoon across the road. Costa was a little too pricey.

She had noticed Danny right away, mostly because he was giving the woman behind the till a piece of his mind. "You need to check it, then," he demanded. "Don't just stand there, accusing me of being a liar. Open the till and check."

Laura had already been sitting down by that point, so she watched the scene unfold like a piece of impromptu theatre. Clearly rattled, the young woman opened the till and clumsily began taking out the money. A young lad came over to help her, printing off a long receipt and checking it over. A queue of people formed behind Danny, each person clearly irritated, yet reluctant to intervene or join the scene. Laura surmised that the young man had tried to pull a fast one with his change but had been caught out. Now he was posturing to save face, trying to intimidate the young girl that dared accuse him. Despite her misgivings, however, Laura found her eyes lingering on the young man as she sipped her tea. His sculpted shoulders bulged through the back of his T-shirt and his thick forearms flexed as he stood there with his hands on his hips.

He must work out.

How tall is he? Six foot?

The only sound for the next two minutes was the clink of hurriedly counted change, which eventually led to a gasp when the young woman looked up from the till and grimaced. "You're right, sir. I'm so sorry. The till is five pounds up."

Danny grumbled, but he sounded more relieved than anything else. He seemed to realise he had made a scene, and his cheeks turned red. "It's fine. No harm done. I'm... um... sorry for losing my temper."

"No, sir, it's my fault." The young woman's voice was all tremors and hitches. Her hands were shaking. "Would you like to grab a sandwich, free of charge?"

Danny shook his head. "It's fine. Can I just get my coffee, please?"

"Of course." The young woman handed over his hot drink, saucer and mug rattling in her unsteady hands. Danny took the steaming beverage and turned away, dumping himself down on the table next to Laura's. He huffed and puffed, muttering under his breath. After a moment, he lifted his mug and took a sip, but it was obviously not to his liking, because he immediately put it back down again and tutted. He glanced around, eyes settling on Laura.

What now? Is he going to kick off again?

The young man stood up.

"Everything okay?" Laura asked, intimidated by his looming presence. He radiated a sense of strength and confidence, despite his nerves clearly being frayed.

He smiled at her, and the creases travelled from the corners of his mouth all the way to a pair of sparkling blue eyes. "Is that sugar?" he asked. "Do you mind if I grab it?"

Laura realised he wanted the sugar cellar in the centre of her table. "Oh, um, yeah, of course. I'm not using it right now."

What? *Right now? Like, I intend to use it later?*

That's some smooth talking there, Lor.

"I'll give it right back," he said, and he reached over and grabbed the cellar. Then he immediately fumbled it. The glass cellar thudded against the table, and the lid popped off as though it had been waiting desperately for the chance. Sugar went everywhere. All over Laura.

She gasped and slid backwards on her seat. "Oh, no!"

"Fuck," said Danny, then seemed to regret his outburst. "Sorry. I'm so sorry. Here, let me clean up the mess. I'll clean it all up. The mess." He got down on his hands and knees and frantically started scooping the sugar into his palm from her thigh. He then seemed to realise what he was doing because he stopped and gasped. "What the hell am I doing? I shouldn't be touching you. God, I'm so sorry."

"I-It's fine," said Laura, realising that people were watching – including the young woman behind the till, who now wore a satisfied smirk.

This is so embarrassing.

She wanted the earth to swallow her up, but she also felt bad for the awkward guy who had just been rubbing her leg. He was so frantic and emotional. Propped up on his knees with a handful of sugar, he suddenly seemed comical. Laura couldn't help but laugh. "So, um, what do you plan on doing with that now that you have it?"

Danny looked down at the pile of sugar in his hand and let out a defeated sigh. "I'm having a bad day."

Laura glanced back at the young woman behind the till, who was back to serving customers. "Yeah. I can tell."

"I behaved like an arse, didn't I?" He clamped his hand shut around the sugar and groaned. "My dream is to be one of those suave, calm complainers who gets their point across without raising their voice, but I always end up losing my cool. I get in a tizzy."

She chuckled. "A tizzy."

"Yeah. Emotional, I guess."

"Call it passion," she said, wanting, for some reason, to be on his side. "Anyway, you were right. She got your change wrong and then called you a liar."

He stood up with his handful of sugar. "All the same, I'll apologise to her before I leave. I lost my temper and I'm embarrassed." He rolled his wonderful blue eyes to the side, as if he dared not look directly at her.

"Don't be embarrassed about *that*," said Laura. "Be embarrassed about tipping sugar all over me." She brushed at her thighs. "And then feeling me up afterwards. Hey..."

She narrowed her eyes. "That wasn't your plan all along, was it?"

He was already blushing, but he now positively lit up. "I'm so sorry."

"Stop apologising. It's fine. Hey, you want to grab your coffee and sit with me? I still have ten more minutes. It looks like you need to vent, and I could use a laugh."

Wow. What am I doing?

Laura was rarely so forward, but she felt strangely at ease with this awkward, emotional young man. She wanted to chase that fluttery feeling in her stomach and not let it go.

"So," she said, "want to sit down and amuse me?"

A smile took over his mouth again. His eyes crinkled. "I would really like that, if you're sure you don't mind. Um, just let me clean up this mess first."

"Just leave it. Your friend will clean it up."

He glanced over at the till. "Yeah, she did try to stiff me, after all."

"Exactly."

With a chuckle, he tipped the sugar onto the other table and grabbed his coffee. After brushing his hands against his jeans for a moment, he then sat down with Laura and they started chatting.

She was late returning from her break that day.

Now, that awkward, emotional man was the father of Laura's daughter, and was half-conscious due to blood loss. She wondered how much he had lost, and how much more he could lose. His wrist appeared to have finally stopped bleeding, but he had grown sleepy and confused.

Will he be okay?

Laura looked out of the window at the two strange men. They circled around and around in the road.

Will we *be okay?*

Laura put a hand on Rose's knee and didn't want to let go. Tonight, she and Danny had been bad parents – negligent parents – and it was still unclear just how dire the consequences of that were going to be.

I need Danny to wake up and clean up this mess.

Before it gets any worse.

Chapter Six

Rose woke with a start, crying the moment she opened her eyes. A deep sleeper, she often woke in the middle of the night, confused and afraid. It didn't help that she was now opening her eyes at two thirty in the morning, strapped to a child's car seat. She peered around the gloomy interior with no sign that she recognised or understood where she was. Her little body shuddered and her hands grasped the air.

"Sh-Shut her up," Danny slurred. "Make her quiet."

Laura put a hand on Rose's chest and rubbed. She got in her daughter's face and smiled. "It's okay, sweetheart. Mummy's here. We're in the car. We're going home."

Rose cried for a moment longer, then whimpered, then fell quiet, blinking her eyes and yawning. "I want my bunny."

"Your bunny? Oh..." Laura chewed at her lip. Rose always slept with her stuffed bunny, but in their haste to leave earlier tonight, they had forgotten to give it to her. "It must be in the boot, baby-girl. I'll see if I can get to it." She half turned on the seat and leant over the parcel shelf. You could remove it, but she wasn't immediately sure how.

"What are you doing?" Danny demanded. He spoke like he was half-asleep and irritable. "Stop it."

"Bunny," said Rose, perhaps sensing her father's disagreement. "I want my bunny."

"It's okay, Dan," said Laura. "It'll just take a second to get it."

"No! Stop it. Someone's coming. I think... I think it's the police. Sit back down."

A shot of adrenaline hit Laura's guts, and she whipped back around to look out of the window. "The police are here? Where?"

Danny tapped the glass and yelled. "Officer? I'm sorry. Was I driving too fast?"

Laura frowned. The two dead men – which was how she now thought of them – were moving from the centre of the road towards the Nissan. They had obviously heard Rose's cries, and Danny's yelling was only attracting them further.

There were no police officers anywhere.

What is Danny talking about? Driving too fast? He thinks we've just been pulled over?

"Danny? Look at me."

He frowned but did as she asked, craning his neck to face her in the back seat. She gasped at the sight of him, his face like fine white porcelain, his eyes like two flawed rubies with black smudges at the centre. "I need to get my licence," he said firmly, as if he were in complete control of himself. "Lor, do you have my wallet?"

"Danny, what are you talking about? There are no police officers out there. What's wrong with you?"

His face cracked, teeth on display. "Keep your mouth

shut, always nagging me. Can't a guy get home from work and relax with a few beers?"

She grabbed him by the shoulder and shook him. "Danny, snap the hell out of it. You're seeing things." He was burning up. She could feel the heat from his skin radiating through his shirt.

The two dead men outside stumbled towards the car.

"Just be quiet," he snapped. "Both of you. Let me deal with this."

"Danny, please, listen to me."

He shrugged her hand away and snarled. "Get the fuck off me, Lor. Do what I tell you to do, or else."

Laura recoiled from the anger in his voice. Danny was completely out of it, but his tone was one she'd heard before. Usually, she would exit the room whenever she heard it, but this time she was trapped in a car with him while dead men stalked the road outside.

Danny slumped forward, making a sound not dissimilar to snoring. It took Laura a moment to realise he had passed out, but it was an unexpected relief to have a break from his anger for a moment.

He's got a fever. He doesn't know what's going on.

But he knew he was talking to me, so why was he so mad?

The dead men stumbled to the edge of the road and crashed against the Nissan. Laura couldn't keep herself from yelling out in horror, which caused them to zero in on the rear window. Rose saw the corpses and squealed, which excited them even more. They moaned hungrily and pawed at the glass. The van driver pressed his face up close, settling any question about him being dead. His left eye was missing, revealing a dark chasm where it had once sat. One of his nostrils had torn open, the flap hanging down his cheek. His throat was sliced wide open, sinew spilling out like spaghetti.

Laura hugged Rose against her chest, trying to soothe her enough to keep her from crying. But it was too late. The monsters were outside, and they weren't going away.

Zombies. They're zombies.

If only I had a shotgun or a chainsaw.

She laughed, feeling like she was moments away from going insane – if she hadn't already. Her fear had reached a point where she was no longer panicking, but instead she was growing increasingly numb, like she was in a dream that she was aware of. Perhaps she was seconds away from waking up in her bed, Danny already left for work.

Or maybe this is the end, and I'm about to die.

Somebody, please help us.

Laura jolted as the dead van driver slammed his face against the rear window next to Rose. Each time he did it, the glass pane rattled in its alcove, leaving more chunks of bloody flesh stuck to the surface. The gore slid slowly downwards.

No, the gore isn't sliding downwards. The window is.

Fear turned to dread as Laura realised the window was gradually lowering after every impact. A slither of a gap had already appeared at the top, a centimetre wide.

Damn this crappy old car.

Unless the van driver retreated, the window would continue sliding down. Then, there would be nothing stopping the corpse from grabbing Rose around the throat and yanking her out of the car.

Or climbing inside and attacking us all.

"Danny! Danny, the window is falling open. You need to do something. Danny, wake up."

He was completely out of it, snoring and choking like

his throat was closed off. He may have been suffocating for all she knew, but there was nothing she could do about it now. She needed to protect Rose.

What do I do?

The window fell open another centimetre. More bloody chunks spattered the glass. The other man, the one who had emerged from the back of the van and caused all of this, stumbled against the wing mirror and ripped it clean off. The damage made enough racket to stir Danny, but he mumbled and went back to sleep.

The window lowered another centimetre.

The van driver got his dirty fingers through the gap. The window slid down faster.

"No! No, stay back."

Laura looked around for a way to save her daughter, but there was nothing she could use. They had to get out of there, but if they left, the zombies could chase them until they dropped.

Maybe the car will start. It might have recovered from the crash.

Do cars do that?

Laura scrambled forward between the seats and reached for the ignition key. As she did so, the sleeve of her blouse caught on something and held her in place. She struggled and pulled, frustrated and frantic. Eventually something *clunked* and her blouse freed itself, causing her to tumble forward. She recovered and looked back to see how much time she had left before the dead man reached in and grabbed Rose, but for some reason he was moving away. His face slid along the glass, leaving a horizontal smear.

Laura gasped. "W-We're moving. What the hell?"

She looked down and saw that the handbrake had lifted. It must have been what she had caught her blouse on.

When she had struggled to get free, she had accidentally yanked up the handle and released the brake.

The car rolled forward at little more than walking speed. After the crash, the car's bonnet had been pointing into a dip. That dip had obviously been deep enough to get the Nissan moving.

The car picked up speed, and Laura laughed in disbelief as the dead men appeared in the rear windscreen, giving chase with their arms out in front of them. Gradually, the glow of the rear headlights left them and the darkness swallowed them up. Laura knew it was only a reprieve – the car couldn't roll along indefinitely – but it gave her a few more seconds to think of a way out of this. She grabbed Danny and shook him. "Wake up, Danny. Fucking wake up, will you?"

Danny's eyes snapped open, as red as before and completely unfocused. It caused Laura to gasp, and she yelped when he suddenly lunged for her. For a moment, it seemed like he was going to bite her, but his mouth stayed closed and he stopped himself inches from her face. He blinked several times, then finally focused. "L-Lor? What's happening?"

"The car's rolling. Those men were about to break in. We need to do something before they surround us again."

He frowned. "Th-The men?" His confusion ebbed away, and he suddenly sat straight up in his seat. "Shit, we need to get out of here, Lor. Hold on, let me—"

His words cut off as the Nissan's nose crunched up against a tree. The bonnet lid hopped, bending slightly in the middle. It was a low-impact crash, but Laura wondered why the airbags hadn't deployed. Was it because the engine was off? Or was it another example of their shitty old car being shitty and old? She glanced back out through the rear windscreen and estimated the dead men to be twenty feet behind. Was now a good time to make a run for it? Did they have enough of a head start to dash into the trees and get away? If not now, then when?

Rose started to scream.

We can't stay trapped here. The dead will get inside.

Danny sat still, staring at the tree trunk in front of them. He appeared dazed, and when Laura leant forward, she spotted a trickle of blood running down his forehead. "Shit, did you hit your head?"

"I... I need air." He reached for the door handle.

"What? No! Danny, wait!"

He wasn't listening. He opened his door and stepped out into the chilly night air. Light rain had begun to fall, and it splashed against the windowsill, forming a shallow puddle on the cheap black plastic. Laura knew they needed to make a run for it, but Danny was in no fit state. Only minutes ago, he had been talking to imaginary police officers.

Do I take Rose and run?

What if Danny doesn't follow? I can't leave him here.

"I don't feel well," said Danny. He stopped a few feet away, having left the car door wide open. "I-I don't feel right."

"Get back inside the car," Laura shouted. In the corner of her eye, she saw that Rose's rear window had dropped another two inches, probably because of the impact of the crash. Now there would be no way to keep out the dead groping hands.

"Damn it, Danny, I need your help. We need to get Rose out of here." She hugged her daughter, thankful she'd stopped crying. "We can't stay here."

"Mummy, I'm cold."

Laura kissed her daughter's forehead. "I know, baby-girl."

"I want my bunny."

"I know."

"Want to go home."

She looked at Rose, doing her best to smile normally. "Mummy knows. We'll be home soon, I promise."

I promise.

Danny started retching, bending over as a stream of vomit erupted from his mouth. Laura couldn't see the vomit, but she heard it splatter against the grass. She also heard sounds of moaning getting closer.

They'll be back any second.

Laura grabbed at her hair and yanked until several copper strands came away, wrapped around her trembling fingers. Danny was going to die out there if she didn't do something.

He needs my help.

She opened the car door, exited, and ran around to the Nissan's rear. The dead were a mere ten feet away, and they moaned hungrily when they saw her. Her heart thudded against her chest. Electricity crackled through her skin.

The air was chilly, the rain cool.

Danny glanced around vacantly, a foul-smelling puddle at his feet. Laura grabbed him and moved him towards the car. "Danny, we have to get back inside. Please, hurry."

He looked at her, reddened eyes almost glowing in the dark. "I don't feel good, Lor."

"I know. Let's just get back in the car."

He nodded and moved more quickly when she pulled on his arm.

The two dead men reached the Nissan but became distracted when they spotted Danny and Laura. They didn't seem to notice Rose sitting in the back of the car, but what if they did? Her window was open. They could reach right in and grab her.

Laura whispered. "Danny, come on. We have to get Rose."

He stopped and frowned at her. "Rose is with Grandma."

"No, Rose is in the car. Fucking snap out of it." She grabbed both of his shoulders and shook him. "I need you."

The dead stumbled alongside the car, heading in Laura and Danny's direction. Thankfully, Rose didn't make a sound, but if she did...

"We need to lead them away." Laura shook Danny by the arm. "We need to protect Rose."

Danny shrugged her away and growled. "Get off me."

She turned back towards the car and then glanced at the road. Maybe she could lead the dead men away on her own. But that would mean leaving Rose in Danny's care, which she couldn't rely upon. Maybe she should make it back inside the car and try to keep the window up somehow. Even if she had to use her hands.

Danny took off, marching towards the trees and ranting to himself angrily. She watched him go, wondering what the hell was going on in his head. There was nothing she could do to stop him, so she stood still, in the darkness, with no idea what to do.

The dead men wandered right by her, chasing after Danny. His loud ranting had captured their attention, and they seemed to home in on him with tunnel vision. Laura daren't even breathe, too frightened to move a single inch in case she shifted their attention.

They're moving away. *I can make it back to Rose.*

But Danny's in danger. He doesn't even know where he is.

Laura had no choice. She rushed back to the car and threw herself in beside Rose, who was staring into space and blinking sleepily. Laura glanced at her watch. Now three in the morning.

Just get into the woods, Danny. Get into the woods and don't stop.

Please don't let those things get you.

"This is a nightmare," she told herself. "I want it to end. I just want it to—"

Screeching brakes broke the silence.

A bright light swung across the road as another car arrived at the road.

It came to a sudden stop behind the upturned van. Several people got out.

Chapter Seven

The newcomers chatted amongst themselves over the din of the car stereo. They sounded drunk, excitable. Immature.

"H-Help," said Laura, but it came out as a whisper. After so much screaming, her voice had become a hoarse mumble that was no match for the thudding bass booming from the other car's stereo. "Help us."

The Nissan had rolled about thirty feet off the road, but with its headlights on it must have been easily visible to anyone looking its way. It was only a matter of time before the strangers spotted it, but right now they were focused on the overturned van, peering into its open rear compartment and muttering to one another.

Three of them. Young men. Not much more than teenagers.

They had arrived in a small hatchback with glaring headlights and had left the car idling at the side of the road while they examined the scene. One of the young lads was loud, whooping and whistling with excitement. "Fuck me," he shouted. "Some serious shit went down here tonight."

"Keep your voice down, Stu," said a calmer young man. "We need to see if anybody's hurt."

"Hey," said a third voice, drunk and slurring. "Is that... is that blood all over the road?"

A brief pause, and then the calm voice answered, "Someone must have been injured. I don't see anybody, though."

"Hey, I think there's something moving around in the back of the van."

Laura trembled in the back seat, desperate to be spotted. The anxiety was making her sick, and she couldn't bear it any longer. She leant forward and bashed the horn three times before leaning on it with both forearms. Rose cried out, disturbed by the sudden blaring din, but Laura needed the teenagers to know they were there. Even if it meant alerting the dead.

The teenagers turned towards the side of the road, alerted by the Nissan's horn, but one of them immediately turned back to the van, leaning forward and peering into its open rear compartment. "Um, guys..."

Laura had a bad feeling.

Did he say there was something moving inside?

Oh no.

Something sprang from the back of the van and collided with the gawking teenager. He screamed – a wailing ghost in the dazzling glare of the hatchback's headlights – as a morbidly obese woman set upon him. She seized him by the arms and bit into his neck.

"Help me!"

Laura gasped. *There had been* two *dead people inside the van. Two zombies.*

Unable to stop herself, she clambered out of the Nissan and started yelling. She waved her hands and jumped up and down. "She's dead. That woman is dead. Get away from her."

The other two teenagers glanced in her direction but then ignored her in favour of trying to help their friend. They wrenched him away from the large woman and threw him to the ground behind them. Then one of them threw a hefty punch that rocked the woman back a step. But she recovered quickly. Like a sumo wrestler, she tackled the lad to the ground and knocked the wind out of him. He was too breathless to scream when she started to eat his face.

That left only one young man uninjured. He stood there in the middle of the road, gawping at what was happening all around him like he couldn't believe his eyes. Laura screamed at the top of her lungs to get his attention. "Get away from her. She's dangerous..."

I sound like the van driver. He tried to warn us.

What am I doing? I'll lead the dead right back to Rose.

But I can't let anyone else die because of me. I have to save this boy.

"Get over here," she shouted again. "Hurry! Get away from her."

The young man's expression turned ghastly as both of his friends begged for mercy, one bleeding from the neck, the other having his face eaten off. He appeared desperate to help them but was smart enough not to try. Blessedly, he sprinted away from the road and towards the Nissan.

"That's it!" Laura cried. "Run!"

The young man reached her quickly, and at the exact same time that somebody else did.

Laura screamed as the van driver emerged from the darkness and grabbed her. If the car hadn't been directly behind her, she might've fallen, but she used it to keep herself upright and lifted a knee to put some distance between her and her attacker. "Get away from me. Get away from me!"

The young lad stood frozen, watching in horror. For a moment, Laura thought he would do nothing to help, but then he got a hold of himself and grabbed the van driver from behind. Turning sideways, he twisted and flung the dead man over his hip and onto the wet grass.

With a moan, the dead man rose again, propped up by a broken leg. The young man must have noticed the injured limb, because he delivered a swift kick right to the shin bone that snapped the leg even more grotesquely. The van driver toppled over and this time couldn't get back up. He could only claw his way through the long grass, snatching at them hungrily.

"What the hell is going on?" The young man's eyes looked ready to pop out of their sockets and roll down his cheeks. His voice was shrill but thankfully sober, unlike his former friends. "What on earth is happening here?"

"Zombies," said Laura, strangely calm. Perhaps it was due to the fact she was no longer the most frightened person out on this road. "That man is dead." She watched the van driver crawling through the long, wet grass. The desert boot from his broken leg had slipped off and lay in the nearby grass. "I watched him die."

The young lad shook his head and pulled a face. "Who are you? What are you doing out here?"

"My name's Laura, and all I can say is that my night started with an argument and went downhill from there. I need to get my daughter out of here, now."

"Daughter?" He dodged to the side, more in frustration than fright, as the crawling van driver tried to grab his leg. "Wh-What daughter? What the hell is going on? We need to call an ambulance. My friends—"

"My daughter!"

Rose was crying in the back of the car. In all the panic, her whimpers had become background noise, and it made Laura feel wretched. Both she and the young man heard her now, though, and they both turned to face the Nissan's rear right window.

"She's inside," said Laura. "I need to get her to your car so we can drive out of here and get help."

"But..." The lad turned back to the road, to where his friends were still in the process of dying. "I don't understand what's happening."

Laura gave him a stern look, surprised she could even manage it. "Listen to what I'm telling you, okay? That woman attacking your friends is dead—a real-life zombie. But right now she's distracted, and we have to get the hell out of here. We need to go."

He seemed to accept what she was saying, or at least that she knew more about what was going on than he did. She judged him to be twenty years old or so, and with his stylish black hair and dark eyelashes, he was extremely handsome. What she liked about him most of all, however, was how he was keeping his shit together.

"I hear you," he said, taking a deep breath and appearing to brace himself. "Dead or not, we need to get you and your daughter out of here."

"Thank you." She went to shake his hand, but the van driver reached out to grab her ankle. He let out a hungry moan, but she dodged away with a pissed-off snarl. Now that she finally had a way out of this nightmare, she wouldn't let anything get in her way.

The young man studied the van driver and grimaced. "You really think he's dead? Like in the movies?"

"I don't watch horror movies," she said. "They scare me.

See if you can lead him away from the car while I get my daughter out."

"Um, sure. Okay."

He stepped away to do as she asked, but she stopped him before he could. "Hey, what's your name?"

"Conner. I was the designated driver for tonight. Now I'm wondering if someone spiked my drink."

"I'm sorry, Conner, but this is really happening."

"Something is, that's for sure." He stepped away from the car and called out to the van driver like he was trying to tempt a cautious dog and not a corpse in dark blue overalls. The dead man half crawled, half scrambled after him, his left leg now at a grotesque right angle and dragging beside him in the grass.

Laura opened Rose's door and leaned in to grab her. "Mummy's here, sweetheart."

"I want to go home."

"We're going right now. Come here, baby-girl." She unbuckled her daughter and pulled her out of the car. She then turned to leave, but someone sprinted out of the trees towards her.

"Lor! Lor, I thought I'd lost you. We need to get out of here."

"No shit, Danny. We're leaving right now. Conner has a car."

Danny skidded to a stop beside the Nissan, almost slipping on the wet grass. "Who's Conner?"

"I am." The lad waved from ten feet away, still luring away the crawling van driver.

Someone else came hurrying out of the trees after Danny. It was the original dead man from the van. He shambled after them rapidly, leaning forward and allowing momentum to carry him. His burst-open lips contorted with the chomping of his teeth, and his broken left arm dangled behind him.

Laura clutched Rose tightly, keeping her face buried. "No, no, no. Come on, we need to get to Conner's car before —" Her lungs deflated as she looked towards the road. The obese woman was now back on her feet, having finished her meal. Both of Conner's friends were standing right behind her. They were dead – except not really. All three zombies looked towards the Nissan, moaning in unison.

Conner saw his friends back on their feet and shook his head in confusion. "Stu? Kyle?"

"They're not your friends any more," warned Laura. "They're dead."

"Hey, guys? What are you—" Conner yelped, startled by the van driver grabbing his leg and chomping down on his trainer. He hopped backwards, pulling his foot back and growling with disgust. No damage was done, but a bloody mouth print stained the shiny white leather. "I-I think I'm going crazy. My friends..."

Danny shook his head. "Damn it, they're blocking the road. What should we do?"

Laura looked around, bobbing Rose up and down in her arms. In a couple of seconds, the dead man from the trees would be on them. A couple of seconds after that, the three from the road would corner them. She couldn't believe what she was about to say, but there was no other choice. "Back inside the car. Now!"

They all did as demanded, and they threw themselves back inside the car right as the dead reached it. Immediately, the ghouls surrounded the Nissan and pawed at the windows. Danny locked the doors. At least he had come back to reality. She needed him.

"That window's open," said Conner, pointing behind

him. He was panting in the front passenger seat beside Danny. The *thud-thud-thud* of his car's stereo drifted in through the gap in the back window.

Laura slumped across the rear seat with Rose on her lap. "It's broken. I don't know how to get it back up again."

"Hold on," said Danny, and he pressed the driver's window controls. The back window jutted up and down angrily, jammed in place. Laura leant over and tried to push it back up with her palm, but it wouldn't budge.

The obese woman spotted the gap and shoved a hand through.

Laura screamed and put Rose behind her. The gap wasn't big enough for the woman to get her arm in past the wrist, but her pudgy fingers wriggled inside the car and carried an almighty stench.

Rose squealed.

"Do something, Lor." Danny bashed at the horn, trying to distract the large woman, but it failed. She had fresh meat in her sights. "Do something!"

"Do what?" If she had had a knife, she would bury it in the woman's pudgy hand, but the only thing within reach was Rose's child seat. She bent forward and pressed the button to remove the seat from its base. Lifting it with both hands, she rotated it and shoved it at the open window. It was a tight fit, the chair wedging between Danny's front headrest and the rear seat behind it, but when Laura put all of her weight behind it, it slid into place, blocking the window entirely. Leaning back, she waited to see what would happen next.

The large woman was no longer visible, with the child seat blocking her, and while the chair shook a little as her colossal bulk pressed against it, it stayed firmly in place.

"I... I think it's going to hold." The longer she waited,

the surer she became that the child seat would remain wedged. "It's not moving."

"That's one less problem to deal with," said Conner, with an appreciative nod. The terror in his eyes had fallen from an eleven and settled on a mere eight. His panting had ceased. "Now we have to move on to the next issue." He turned to face Danny, a grim expression on his face. "You do not look well, sir."

Danny took a few quick breaths before speaking. It was a surreal environment in which to hold a conversation, what with a bunch of dead people thumping their meaty fists against the windows, but silence wouldn't do them any favours. They needed to talk through a solution to this. "I'm fine," he said, his voice a note deeper than usual. "There's no time to worry about me."

"I disagree," said Conner. "I'm a medical student, and you clearly need medical attention. Your skin is grey. Your eyes are red. I think you may be septic. Are you wounded?"

"You might say that." He held up his bandaged wrist. Blood caked Laura's torn sleeve. "I got bit by one of those psychos out there."

Conner wrinkled his nose. "I don't even need to look to know that wound is infected. Take off that bandage, it's filthy." He reached into his pocket and pulled out a set of car keys. On the attached keyring was a small plastic bottle. "Thanks to studying at a hospital during a pandemic, I don't go anywhere without alcohol gel. It won't do much, but I can disinfect your wound at least."

"It's fine," said Danny, pulling his wrist away. "How do you even have your car keys? Your radio is still playing over there. Your high beams are still on."

Conner shrugged. "Keyless ignition. Welcome to 2021."

Danny rolled his eyes. "Daddy buy you a nice new car, did he?"

"Yes, as it happens, but that doesn't really matter right now, does it? I want to help you."

"Just let him clean your wound," said Laura. "You've been acting weird, Danny. We need to take care of you. Rose needs you at your best."

Danny groaned unhappily, but he relented and offered his wrist out, allowing Conner to remove the filthy bandage. The polyester had melded with his flesh, but he didn't flinch when it peeled free. The wound no longer bled – a relief – but it looked and smelled terrible. It was the colour of smashed plums – yellows and reds mixed together – and sodden with stinking fluids that smelled like feet and rancid chicken. Laura felt a bulge in her throat.

"This is bad," said Conner. He seemed reluctant to touch the wound, but he held Danny's wrist with one hand and used the other to squeeze the tiny bottle of alcohol gel over the puncture wound where the infection seemed to be worst. Once again, Danny gave no indication he was in any pain, and Laura couldn't see that as a good sign. She was just glad he was lucid again. Perhaps his fever had broken. The redness of his eyes had faded, and a slither of his normal sky-blue showed through.

"Doesn't it hurt, babe?" asked Laura, wishing she could whisk him away to A & E. "It looks terrible."

Danny shrugged. "It hurt at first. Not any more."

Conner placed the back of his hand against Danny's forehead. "You're warm, but I don't think you have a temperature. Do you feel sick at all? Dizzy? Who's the Prime Minister?"

"A fat Tory with too much money. And, no, I don't feel sick or dizzy. I feel fine. Just a little spaced out. Sleepy."

Conner nodded. "Then let's hope for the best. Okay, on to the next problem, which is that we're trapped inside a car and surrounded by"—he looked at Laura and frowned—"by what you say are dead people. Have you called for help? My phone is in my car. Do either of you have a signal?"

"We don't have our phones," said Laura.

"What? Neither of you? Who doesn't have a mobile phone these days?"

Danny grunted. "She threw my phone out of the window."

"Because you threw mine first!"

"To stop you crying to Daddy."

"I was trying to make things right after your freak-out. Maybe if you—"

Conner put his hands up. "Great, so we're screwed. My friends and I stopped to help with what we thought was a traffic accident. Now, they're out there, walking around with wounds that need immediate attention and no way to call for help – and don't tell me they're dead, because that's utterly insane. One of you needs to talk sense and tell me what's going on, because I demand to know the truth. Start at the beginning – and be quick about it because I don't think we have much time."

Laura broke out in hysterical sobbing. She'd been holding it back for a while and had now lost the strength to contain it. Conner's sudden stern tone, along with the mention of the crash, sent her right back to the start of this night. It reminded her how irresponsible she and Danny had been, and how they were solely to blame for this. She tried to talk, but her words came out as an incomprehensible squawk. Despite his age, Conner was just so... angry.

Who can blame him?

His friends are dead because of us.

"For Christ's sake," said Danny, groaning. "That won't help, will it, Lor? Calm the fuck down."

Conner sighed, then reached back to place a hand on Laura's knee, much to Danny's visible displeasure. "I'm sorry for snapping. I think I'm still in the throes of shock. This is a lot to deal with, but deal with it we shall. Let's just put our heads together, yes?"

The obese woman thumped a fist against Laura's window and made everyone flinch. Her sobbing had excited the dead woman, yet Laura still couldn't stop. She nodded in reply to Conner's words and he removed his hand from her leg. Danny glared at him.

Laura tried to catch her breath. "This... This is so... fucked up."

"No arguments here," said Conner. He was visibly trembling, yet he behaved calmly. In fact, he seemed determined. "Can we switch off the lights in here?"

"Why?" asked Danny.

"Because I feel like we're on display, and I don't want to make it easy for our enemies to see what we're up to. If they're locked in some kind of psychosis, they might even forget we're in here."

Danny grunted, but he reached up and switched off the interior lights. It surprised Laura to find that she preferred the dark. It was like being invisible, wrapped up in shadow. Rose cried out at first, but she did settle.

Laura managed to stop crying, which was a relief to everyone. They weren't in immediate danger. The remaining three windows held.

"They're not psychotic," Laura muttered, wanting to fill the silence. "They're dead."

Conner pointedly ignored her. He twisted around in his seat and smiled at Rose, who could probably only barely make him out. "So," he whispered, voice competing with the thudding bass of the nearby car stereo, "what's your name, little lady?"

"You can answer the man," said Laura, squeezing her daughter's tiny hand to reassure her.

"R-Rose Mayweather."

Conner's face lit up. "Rose? What a beautiful name. Have you ever seen a rose? They're the prettiest flower in the world."

Rose beamed. "We have pink ones in our garden."

"Wow. I would love to smell them."

"You can."

"Really? Are you inviting me to come and play at your house?"

Rose nodded. Laura gave Conner a smile, which she wasn't sure he could see in the dark. Danny slumped in his seat, staring ahead and saying nothing. She wondered if he was going to be okay. Would his sickness get worse or better? What would happen if you didn't take medicine for an infection? Would his body fight it? Conner had said he might be septic.

"I'm sorry about your friends," said Laura, watching as one of the dead teenagers walked around in front of the bonnet. He was young and blond and handsome. What kind of life would he have had ahead of him? A good one, probably. "Were your friends doctors too, Conner?"

"I'm not a doctor. I'm halfway through a medical degree, but I train at a hospital two days a week. And to answer your question, no, Stu and Kyle are most certainly not doctors. I grew up with them – lived on the same road – but we took very different paths in life. Stu hasn't held a job for more than a couple of months at a time, and Kyle is just a landscaper."

"*Just* a landscaper?" said Danny. "Beneath you, is it? Only doctors and lawyers worthy of your respect? I'm just a plumber, mate, so you might want to avoid touching me."

Conner cleared his throat awkwardly. "You're right. That was crass of me. I only meant it in that Kyle could do anything he wants in life if he were to put a little more effort into things. He's a smart guy when he wants to be, but a little directionless."

"He *was* a smart guy," said Danny. "Your mate's dead. They're *all* dead."

"I refuse to believe that. They're sick, and they need treatment."

"And what would you recommend, Doc?" Danny turned his head and smirked. "Tell me, what disease have you learned about that can do this to a person? Your friends were normal ten minutes ago, right? Oh look, here's one of them now with his throat torn out. Still say he's not dead?"

Conner watched his friend walk by and failed to give an answer. He failed because there was no argument he could make. Laura knew how hard a thing it was to accept that this nightmare was real, but it was the truth. The people outside were dead.

And if we don't find a way to escape, we're all going to end up the same way.

Chapter Eight

Things were bad—and continued to get worse. "I need the toilet," said Laura, suffering with the large glass of wine still in her bladder. Now that she was aware of the need to pee, it grew pressing. "I'm bursting."

Danny groaned. "Yeah, I need to go, too. Suppose we'll just have to piss ourselves."

Rose was still awake, staring ahead dozily in the darkness that was broken only by the moonlight and the nearby headlights of the other vehicles. Laura didn't like Danny swearing in front of her, but she supposed it didn't matter as much right now. If Rose hadn't already been traumatised, it would be a miracle.

My poor baby. I can't believe I've put her in so much danger.

Laura doubled over and pressed her knees together. "Do we have any plastic bottles? Coke cans?"

"No," said Danny. "I cleaned the car out before we left home yesterday."

"What about in the boot?"

Danny shrugged. He seemed irritated, jaw tensing at the jowls. "You packed the bags, Lor. Did you pack anything we can piss in?"

Conner shushed them both. "Stop bickering."

Danny scowled at him. "Who you think you're talking to? If you want to go and—"

Conner shushed him again, this time with a finger against his lips. "Be quiet! I've been watching them out there. They're leaving."

Danny's face turned sour, but Laura didn't give him a chance to throw a tantrum. She leant forward and spoke with Conner. "What do you mean, they're leaving?"

"They've been moving slowly away from us," he said, pointing. "Look!"

Laura couldn't see the road from the rear seats because of the child seat jammed into the window, so she shuffled forward and peered across Danny. It was true. The dead people were moving away, now closer to the road than the Nissan. "Why are they leaving?"

"It's my car radio," said Conner, referring to the thudding stereo that was yet to die. "The noise is attracting them. I think they've forgotten we're in here."

"Because we turned off the lights and stayed quiet," said Laura. "You were right."

Danny grunted. "They're still out there, so unless you have a way to kill them, I wouldn't get too excited."

"How do you kill something that's already dead?" asked Laura. "Our only hope is to escape."

Conner nodded. "I'll go. I'll run and get help."

"No," said Laura. "Not yet. If they've gone away, we're safe. Maybe we should wait for help."

"But if they come back—"

"No, please. If we're going to leave, fine, but we should do it together. Danny is getting back his strength."

Conner looked at Danny curiously. It was true that he was looking healthier – his eyes were no longer red and his breathing was steady – but he was still deathly pale.

"I just need a little while longer," said Danny. He let out a sigh and shook his head. "I'll get us out of here somehow. You can't run out on your own, kid. The nearest town is a few miles back, at least. It would take at least an hour for you to bring back help. We're safe, so let's not take any risks."

Conner nodded. "Okay, so we delay our escape. We still have another problem to deal with, though."

Laura raised an eyebrow. She liked the way Conner ordered things, making each issue separate and manageable. Even Danny seemed to have a begrudging respect for his calmness. "What problem?"

"We still need to go the bathroom."

Laura grimaced. "Right. It's not going to go away. I need to go."

"Perhaps..." Conner pulled at his fingers thoughtfully. "Perhaps if we're quiet – and if someone keeps watch – we can creep out and go on the grass. The car will keep us hidden from the road."

"I'm not going outside," said Laura. "No way."

"Then you'll have to piss your knickers," said Danny, the hint of a smile on his pasty face.

"Stop swearing," Laura hissed. "Rose is awake. She can hear you."

Danny grumbled, but he apologised and changed the subject. "Those things are back on the road for now. How many of them are there?"

"Five," said Laura. She had already familiarised herself

with the number of threats to her daughter. The zombie with the broken arm. The van driver. Conner's two friends. The fat woman. "There are five of them out there."

Danny took a moment, moving his face closer to the window. "I only see four. There's one missing."

"The van driver," said Laura. "He can't stand up. He has a broken leg."

"Then he could be anywhere."

"I'll go out and look," said Conner. "And before you argue, I can jump straight back inside if I need to. The worst danger is on the road."

We could lead the dead back to our car, thought Laura. *But I really do need to pee.*

Facing no argument, Conner carefully pushed open the front passenger door and placed a foot outside on the grass. The Nissan's bonnet was still scrunched up against the tree, so Conner exited right up against the edge of the woods. Cold air swirled inside the car, causing Rose to tremble. Laura put a hand on her daughter's chest. "It's okay, baby-girl."

"Want my bunny."

Laura shushed her. "I know, honey."

"Cold."

"Let me hold you."

"Bunny."

Laura looked around for a solution, and found a compromise. She reached forward and plucked the Mr Bump off the rear-view mirror and handed it to Rose.

Rose took the toy and smiled. "Bumpy Man."

"Yes, Bumpy Man will look after you."

She hugged the Mr Bump against her cheek and seemed content for the time being.

Danny grunted in the front seat. He stared out the

window and watched Conner with something approaching disdain on his face. Danny didn't like the kid, that much was clear.

Laura struggled to breathe, a mixture of chilliness and trepidation. Conner was outside. The dead people were still on the road, gathering around his car. The fat woman was currently trying to crawl into the driver's seat, presumably searching for the source of the music.

They can't think. They can only react.

"Okay, it's clear," said Conner, poking his head back inside the car. "Who's first? I'll keep watch."

"I'll go," said Danny. "I want to make sure it really is safe."

Laura didn't know how much longer she could hold her bladder, but it wouldn't hurt to let Danny check things out as well. She pressed her knees together while her husband slid out through the driver's door and crept into the trees. When he began peeing, he released a loud shudder.

Be quiet. Has he forgotten we're being hunted?

Conner glanced in at Laura with a concerned expression, a thin-lipped smile that seemed to say: *Can you shut your husband up?* Laura tried to convey a message back: *If only I could.*

Mercifully, Danny returned to the car without further incident, and once inside, he closed the driver's door quietly. He shuddered in his seat. "Christ! I needed that."

"Is it safe out there?" asked Laura.

"Yeah. Go do what you need to do. Hey, I'm feeling much better. We can leave soon. I'll get us out of this."

"Just take it easy." She reached forward and placed a hand on his shoulder. "I'll be right back, okay? Keep an eye on Rose."

"She's fine. Hurry up."

Conner was still keeping watch outside. He opened the back door for her and then reached in to help her slide out. Rose whimpered, but Danny turned around to soothe her. Laura gasped as she stepped out into the cold beneath a light drizzle that was only partly obstructed by the branches overhead. The grass beneath her feet was slippery and long, and in several places it rose knee-high. She found a bare patch of ground that was more mud than anything else and prepared to do her business.

Conner stared at her blankly, but blushed when her need for privacy dawned on him. "Oh, sorry. I'll turn my back. Call out if you need me."

She smiled and patted him on the arm. "I think I've got this."

"Sure. Watch out for snakes."

"What? That's not funny."

He grinned. "I couldn't help myself."

"Turn around, young man." She was smiling but tried to look stern. Once he had, she took two steps into the trees and undid her buttons. As soon as she had yanked down her jeans and underwear, the pee came almost immediately, almost before she had even managed to squat. The stream hit the mud like a pressure washer, and a wave of relief washed over her.

Something touched her foot. For a moment, she assumed it was her own clothing, or perhaps a twig breaking underfoot, but then she heard a moan. With a start, she tumbled backwards and let out a scream. The dead van driver reached out to grab her, forcing her to scurry backwards, jeans tangled around her ankles.

Broken teeth gnashed at the air. Hands wrapped around her ankles.

She screamed. "No! Get away!"

The van driver lunged.

His head thudded against the mud beside her knee. Something protruded from his temple.

Laura gasped for air. Her fingers dug into the wet grass behind her.

Conner yanked the tree branch out of the van driver's skull with a sickening squelch. He was panting slightly. "Laura? Are you okay?"

She nodded breathlessly, heart pounding. He reached out, and she took his hand, hoisting herself to her feet. Too startled to be embarrassed, she tugged up her jeans and clumsily fastened the buttons. The van driver moaned and snatched at her ankles again. Blood and brains oozed from the hole in the side of his head.

"Damn it!" Conner rammed the branch down again, creating a new hole in the dead man's skull. He yanked it free and stomped with his trainer, cracking the bleeding skull further. The van driver continued to moan and reach out, undeterred.

"You can't kill the dead," said Laura. "You can't—"

Danny called out to them from inside the car. His words didn't register for a moment, but then Laura glanced towards the road and saw the dead people approaching.

Conner stamped on the van driver's skull for a second time, and when it again failed to put an end to the ghoul, he lost his temper and bent at the knees, preparing to deliver a stomp with both feet. But his launch was awkward, and his left foot slipped on the piss-soaked mud. His ankle rolled over and he yelped in pain. His balance deserted him.

Laura caught him before he crumpled and kept him on his feet. "Back inside the car. Now!"

He gritted his teeth in pain and nodded, then hurried back inside the Nissan with Laura. Rose was crying, and Danny was swearing, but everyone was okay. The interior lights came on briefly, but then faded. Laura held Rose in her arms, hugging her and whispering sweet nothings. "Mummy loves you, honey-bug."

"Love you, too, Mummy. Are you sad?"

Laura realised she was crying. "I'm just happy because you're such a beautiful girl. Tomorrow, we're going to go to the park and eat ice cream, okay?"

"Can we buy sweeties?"

"Of course we can. You need to be quiet now, okay, sweetheart?"

Rose smiled wearily. At Nanny and Grandad's she had stayed up well past bedtime, and since then she had been woken constantly. Laura wanted nothing more than for her sweet daughter to sleep through all this.

Danny shushed everyone and slid down in his seat.

The dead arrived. They pawed at the glass, laying siege once again. Their dead eyes stared blindly. They didn't blink. Nor did they breathe.

Everyone inside the car kept still, remained silent. Laura rocked Rose to and fro.

After a few minutes, the dead wandered away, lured once more by the noise coming from Conner's car radio.

We're safe inside the car. As long as we're quiet and we keep the lights off.

Someone will come. Someone will save us.

Like Conner and his friends? Whoever stops on this road is going to end up dead. Dead and walking around. This road is cursed.

"I need to go for help," said Conner. He grasped his twisted ankle and winced. "We can't wait here hoping for the best. I'm going to go."

"You're hurt, Conner. Just rest your ankle. We'll figure something out."

"No!" He suddenly sounded panicked. "I-I have to get out of here. This... This is crazy. They really are dead, aren't they? My friends are dead. Kyle... Stu..."

"I don't know how it's possible," said Laura, "but, yes, they're dead. I'm sorry."

Conner pinched his nose and closed his eyes. After a moment, he shook his head and stared at her. "How is this possible?"

"I don't know."

"Those things ate my friends. And then my friends got back up and tried to eat *us*."

Danny held his arm up. "The bastards already made a good start on me."

Conner opened his mouth to speak, but he closed it again and instead said nothing. He fell silent, thoughtful, continuing to massage his ankle and wince periodically.

"Thank you for saving me out there," said Laura. "He must have been hiding in the trees."

"You wouldn't have needed saving," said Danny, "if Eton had kept watch properly."

"His name is Conner," said Laura. "Show some respect, Danny."

Conner sighed. "He's right. I'm sorry. I let you down. As soon as I realised you were in danger, I found the thickest branch I could and buried it in that thing's head. But it's still out there, crawling around like I barely touched it. You were right, Laura, you can't kill the dead." He chuckled, at odds with his tone. Then he shook his head as though he were trying to shake off an unwanted thought.

Laura frowned. "What is it?"

"Just a tale I remember reading about. I think it was in a

book about medieval medicine. It wasn't on the recommended reading list, but when I saw it at the university library, it called out to me. I've always enjoyed the odd dashing of weird history."

"How delightful," said Danny, placing his head back against the rest and closing his eyes.

Laura grumbled. The situation was already dire, but Danny's constant grumbling was only making it worse. "Be quiet, Dan. You're not helping."

"Don't tell me to be quiet. You got us into this mess."

"How? How the hell did I cause this?"

He didn't answer or even open his eyes. His jaw was tense once again. His one hand squeezed the steering wheel tightly. Across his lap, his wounded wrist glistened.

"Can I please tell my story?" Conner sniffed. "It might pass the time."

Laura raised an eyebrow. "What story? The one from the medical book?"

"I suppose it was more of a history book, but yes. Anyway, this tale I read concerned a village during the time of the Black Death. Despite the bubonic plague being everywhere, this particular village remained completely unaffected. Not a single villager there had caught the plague, even after travelling to and from infected places. Soon, and as an unfortunate consequence of the times, accusations of black magic and deals with the devil began to circulate. Now, England wasn't as bad as America in those days – there was no burning people at the stake or drowning witches – but the villagers were, however, made into pariahs. No one would trade with them, or even allow them to travel on the public roads. They quickly starved, and eventually turned to highway robbery to survive, killing those who had forsaken them."

"What does that have to do with our current situation?" asked Danny. He actually sounded interested.

"They met a man on the road one day," Conner continued. His tone had become almost conspiratorial, like he was letting them in on a secret. "Bedraggled and plague-ravaged, the stranger was days away from death. The villagers, still possessing the last vestiges of their humanity, decided to give this diseased man the mercy of a quick end. They brutally set about his head and body with clubs, striking him repeatedly, but he kept getting up, no matter how badly they beat him."

"How is that possible?" asked Laura.

Conner smiled, like an old man taking a child's question. "The book posited that an elderly man close to death can be as strong as the healthiest of young men. Adrenaline, and other chemicals, provide the body with a last burst of life that can make a dying man unexpectedly vigorous. It took those villagers over one hour to beat the dying, diseased man to death, and in doing so, they were clawed and bitten several times over. Within days, the entire village had caught the plague, and the village scribe jotted warnings in his diary about an undead man on the road with the power to spread death and disease with bites and scratches. A zombie... of sorts."

"And this was in a book about medicine?" Laura pulled a face.

Conner shrugged. "Medical superstition throughout the ages. Anyway, I think the lesson to be learned is that no place is safe from disease, and that it only takes a single person to bring devastation to an entire population. I also believe it tells us that a man remains very much alive until the precise moment death takes him. More so even."

"So we might be in a shit situation," said Danny, eyes

still closed, head still back, "but we're not dead until we're dead."

"Precisely," said Conner. "We will find the strength we need, even in our darkest hours."

"Or," said Laura, "maybe the story was taken from a plague victim's fevered writings and means nothing at all."

Conner chuckled. "You're probably right. Anyway, I often wonder about that sickly man on the road. Who was he? Why was he wandering alone in such a state?"

Danny ran his hands through his hair, slick with sweat. "I'm feeling better. I think we should make a run for it."

"The van driver is still out there," said Laura. "We could stumble right into him. Conner, how's your ankle? Do you think you can run?"

"It's just a sprain, but I can feel it swelling. It'll slow me down, at the very least."

"It has to be me alone," said Danny. "I'll head into the woods and find help."

"What if you get lost?" Laura shook her head, her mind conjuring the worst. "It's almost four in the morning and those woods might go on for miles. You could end up lost, or you might pass out from your wounds. You're still not right, Dan. What if you keel over before you make it ten feet?"

"I'm fine, Lor. And if not me, then who?"

Laura glanced at Rose lying across her lap and was glad to see that she was asleep once again. "I'll go."

"No way." Danny clutched the wheel with both hands and finally opened his eyes. "You're not going out there, Lor. You can't."

"Why not? Why can you go but not me? I'm the only one who isn't injured. Look, I'm going outside, okay? But not to run aimlessly through the woods."

Conner raised an eyebrow. "Then where?"

She looked at him. "To your car. You said you have a mobile phone inside."

"I do. It's attached to a holder on the dashboard. I make Uber runs for extra money, and I use my phone as a satnav."

"Then I'm going to get it and call for help," said Laura. "This will all be over."

Danny tutted. "You've lost the plot, Lor. Those things are surrounding Conner's car because of that sodding music blasting out. How are you planning to get inside?"

"With a distraction."

Conner nodded immediately, as if he understood. "We can blare the horn. Get their attention."

"No. I won't have you bringing them back to Rose. Danny, do you think you can lure them away from the road without getting yourself eaten?"

He didn't seem to like the idea, but she had phrased it as a challenge, which she knew would prod at his ego. He chewed the inside of his cheek before nodding. "I'll lead them towards the trees, then sneak back to the car. But if they see you, Lor, you get your arse back in the car, do you hear me? I'll never forgive myself if you get hurt. If I hadn't dragged us away tonight..." He shook his head and closed his eyes tightly. "Just be careful, okay? I love you too much to lose you."

Laura was taken aback. Danny was himself again, speaking to her with love and concern, with no hint of the fevered confusion he had been exhibiting since being bitten. She realised then how much she had missed him. How much she loved him.

Despite his recovery, Danny still didn't look fully right. Small red veins crisscrossed his cheek, and his eyes were so moist that they were almost weeping. When she studied him closely, she saw his entire body was trembling.

I need his help. I can't get to the other car while the dead are on the road.

Am I actually going to do this?

I have to. There's no one else. I have to do it for Rose.

"Okay," she said. "I'm ready."

Chapter Nine

There was a fairground in her guts, carousels and Ferris wheels going round and around. But she couldn't let her fear rule her. Her entire life, she had chosen the safe options – the path of least responsibility. First, she had lived beneath her father's strict rule, never having to think for herself or worry about taking care of herself. Then, she had married Danny, another headstrong man who liked to take charge. But her father wasn't here and Danny was injured, so no one was going to get her out of this.

No more sitting back and doing nothing. Time to take charge.

Oh shit, oh shit, oh shit.

"I'll go first," said Danny, wrapping his fingers around the door handle. "Remember, come straight back if you're in trouble."

She nodded. "You too."

Danny opened the door and crept out onto the grass, stumbling unsteadily towards the trees. The Nissan's dangling headlight flickered, causing him to come in and out of view like an image from an old, barely working television.

"You sure you want to do this?" asked Conner, turning to look at her. His dark hair was a mess from where he'd been clutching it in his pain. Even now, he winced as he spoke. "My ankle isn't that bad. I can go."

"Just look after Rose, okay? If she wakes up, tell her Mummy will be right back."

"What if she cries?"

"Then sing Disney songs to her."

Conner cleared his throat. "I, um... I'm not sure I know any. Maybe that one from *Frozen*."

"That's all you need. Thanks, Conner. I'll buy you a beer after all this is over."

"I don't drink alcohol. I'll take a rooibos tea, though."

"That's weird, but okay." She put a hand on the door handle and paused for a moment to steel her nerves. Then, she exited the car against the tree line, hidden from the road. The dead wouldn't see her unless she broke cover, so she ducked down and headed around to the Nissan's boot. She stayed there for several moments, waiting for Danny to start his distraction. She couldn't see him, nor hear him, and time went on.

And on.

What is he doing?

Come on, Danny.

"Hey! Hey, you wankers. Over here!"

Laura flinched at the broken silence, quickly panicking now that the plan was in motion. Soon, she would have to break cover and head for the road – the road stained with blood and fogged with the stench of death.

Movement up ahead. The dead were on the move. It reminded Laura that there was one still unaccounted for, so she quickly turned in search of the van driver. He was crawling in the grass a little way away, groping around blindly. His skull was flattened, his eyeballs squashed beyond use. Only the walking dead were a threat right now.

She waited in cover for almost a full minute and then started creeping forward. She kept low, fingertips brushing against the grass. The dead didn't see her. They shambled after Danny, lured by his shouting. Conner's car was directly in front of her, sitting outside the glow of both the Nissan and the van's headlights, but well-lit by its own. Its interior lights were off, but the radio still blared. It was a small modern car – a well-off student's runaround – and the phone inside would be their salvation.

She scurried forward, the adrenaline in her system refusing to let her dawdle. She reached the edge of the road, where broken shards of glass and chunks of plastic littered the tarmac. The van lay on its side to her left, Conner's car to her right. She glanced behind her, checking on the dead. They remained distracted, heading across the grass and towards the woods. She spotted three of them clearly, shambling together in a line.

Courage caused her to rise, and she hurried to Conner's car. Up close, the thudding music was wince-inducing. It brought back her headache with a vengeance.

Both of the hatchback's front doors were open wide. Laura lowered her head and threw herself in through the passenger side, clambering onto the seat. She didn't expect it when the obese woman reached out and grabbed her. The dead glutton had wedged herself half inside the car and half out, having entered through the driver's side. Her colossal bulk wobbled between the steering wheel and the driver's seat, which had been slid forward, probably when Conner had first stopped and allowed his other friend to get out of the back. When the dead woman spotted Laura, she let out a moan and reached out with one hand. Her fingernails hung loose from their bloody beds, attached by strands of slippery gore. A hungry mouth leaked dark, chunky fluids all over the centre console.

Laura screamed and tried to get back out of the car, but the dead woman grabbed the remaining sleeve of her blouse. The stitching tore and then, just like earlier, held strong. She couldn't pull away. The other woman was too strong, and the only thing keeping her diseased teeth away from Laura's flesh was the fact she was wedged.

Laura tugged and twisted, not daring to punch the dead woman in case she got bitten. Also, she had never punched a person in her life and wasn't sure she could do it. Instead, she tried to use her legs to force herself backwards out of the open door, but that was no use either. Panicking, she twisted and kicked, lashing out at the dead woman's face with her short black ankle boots. She rammed a heel right into the corpse's mouth, knocking loose several decayed teeth. Then she kicked again and again until the dead woman finally recoiled. There was a vile *slopping* sound as the woman's stomach tore open against the steering wheel, and her guts spilled everywhere. Laura kicked again, this time with both feet, and forced the massive dead woman out of the car.

Finally free, Laura's first instinct was to escape and run back to the Nissan, but she stopped herself. She'd risked herself for a reason.

The phone.

She searched for Conner's mobile and quickly found the holder. But the gore-soaked holder was empty. The dead woman's bulk must have knocked the phone loose.

So where is it? Where the fuck is it?

The bass from the car stereo pounded in her head. Her heart thudded against her chest. A stitch tore into her ribs. She was running on empty.

Don't give up.

She glanced into the footwell, attracted by the glint of a glass screen. With a relieved gasp, she reached down to grab it, lowering herself and stretching out her arm.

The dead woman lunged back into the driver's seat and grabbed Laura's blouse again, this time by the scruff of the neck. Laura pulled away, squealing, but the pudgy dead hand clutched her too tightly. She couldn't get away.

She's going to eat me.

Desperate, Laura forced herself backwards with all she had. Her body moved backwards, but her arms stayed behind, rising above her head until she slipped right out of her blouse. She tumbled backwards and landed on the road half-naked. A yelp escaped her lips as the gravel chewed up her back, but she quickly leapt to her feet and got moving. The dead woman breast-crawled across the front seats, trying to get at Laura. Her corpulent tummy shed flesh into the footwells, and any chance of getting to Conner's phone disappeared.

What now? This was our best chance, and I screwed it up. I can't do anything right.

Wedging herself again, the dead woman's leaking flab pressed against the car horn. The blaring din was louder even than the car's stereo, and Laura knew it would act as a beacon. She glanced back towards the tree line, and while she didn't see the dead in the darkness, she heard their moans. Danny squawked at them relentlessly, his voice growing louder and louder, but it was clear that he was beginning to fret.

He's losing them. They're coming back towards the road.

It would take several minutes for the obese woman to remove herself from Conner's car, so Laura had a moment to think about what to do next. Her only instinct was to run, but she couldn't abandon Rose. She wouldn't.

Never.

I have to make it back to the car before it's too late.

She set off running, heading back to the safety of the Nissan. Back to Rose.

But she couldn't make it.

The dead re-entered the glow of the Nissan's headlights. When they saw Laura racing towards them, they reached out to her and moaned. Her path to safety now blocked, she stopped at the edge of the road. Danny followed behind the dead people, trying to regain their attention. They ignored his insults, focused only on Laura.

"Get out of here," Danny shouted to her. "I can't stop them." He grabbed one of Conner's undead friends by the shoulder and spun the dead lad around, but even that didn't get the zombie's attention. It was like Danny had suddenly become invisible. It didn't make any sense.

Laura back-pedalled again and almost tripped. She kept trying to find a way forward, a route back to the Nissan, but it was too dangerous. The dead were clumsy, but they were also quick. They almost seemed to fall towards her, upper halves tilted in her direction. Her only option was to make a run for it and try to find help – even if it was miles away.

Maybe there's a farm or a cottage nearby. I just need a phone or a car.

Or an exorcism kit.

Laura turned to run, but she found herself face to face with the fat woman who had slid free of Conner's car quicker than she had expected. Laura hadn't even noticed that the car horn had been silent. The woman's massive torso was a sagging mess of flesh and excrement, with several lengths of entrails swinging by her legs. The stench was like every rotten smell mixed up inside a septic tank – shit, pus, and disease. Pain. Suffering. Death. The pungent, eye-watering effluvium of hell.

Laura fought to keep her gorge down as she staggered dizzily away from the dead woman and back into the centre of the road. Behind her, the three male corpses stalked towards her. Even if she ran now, she would eventually run out of breath, and the dead would continue to chase her to the ends of the Earth.

I need to hide. They go away when they can't see or hear you.

Laura glanced back towards Conner's car but didn't think she could make it inside with the obese woman in her way. The only other thing out on the road was the upturned van. Its back door was still open. Was it empty inside?

Or are there more zombies?

The dead were getting closer, spreading out and surrounding her. Time was running out.

"Run!" Danny yelled, and then doubled over, vomiting ferociously into the grass. He sank to his knees, groaning in agony. Behind him, the Nissan rocked on its springs as Conner leapt out to help him. He gathered Danny back to his feet and led him back to the car. Before he disappeared back inside, Conner looked across the roof at Laura. "Forget about us," he yelled. "Get to safety."

But there was no safety.

And Rose needed her mummy.

Laura looked again towards the van, seeing it as her only option. She then spotted something else. The van driver's phone was still lying on the ground from when Danny had failed to grab it.

Can I get to it? Can I make a call?

Laura sprinted up the road, the wind chilling her exposed midriff. Her back was stinging, cut up from the road, yet the pain made her feel alive, put her in touch with her body. She reached the van in seconds and dropped to her knees, scooping up the phone and glancing at the screen. It was like nothing she'd ever seen before. Not a touchscreen, but an old-fashioned handset – more like a radio than a mobile phone. She thumbed at the buttons, causing a tiny low-res screen to light up.

The fat woman had followed and now leapt forward to grab Laura, but Laura flinched and rolled away. She launched herself up off her knees and back onto her feet. She had a phone.

But the dead were coming at her from every direction.

Laura turned on her heels, seeking an escape. Doing the only thing she could think of, she ducked towards the upturned van and entered through the open rear door. Darkness met her.

She prayed that was all.

Chapter Ten

It was dark inside the van, and when Laura reached out and pulled up the door, it became pitch-black. She stood there in silence, panting... waiting. She waited for groping hands to seize her in the darkness, for teeth to sink into her flesh, but nothing happened. A few seconds passed, fists started to beat against the rear doors, but they remained closed. No one attempted to twist the handles or fiddle with the locks. The zombies, once again, proved themselves mindless.

Her heartbeat slowed from a sprint to a sweaty jog. She turned a circle, head brushing against the ceiling that was actually one of the van's side walls. Groping around in the darkness, she feared touching flesh that was not her own, but slowly she realised she was alone. The interior was cramped and filled with fixtures and fittings. Her foot brushed against all manner of things on the ground. At the rear of the space, she felt metal bars.

A cage? Those dead people must have been locked inside here. The crash caused the cage to open and let them free.

This was a goddamn zombie delivery service. DeadEx. Where were they being taken?

Laura's mind teemed with conspiracies, of military projects, medical trials, government cover-ups, and worse. What could make the dead walk? An accident? An aberration of nature? Or was it something beyond her understanding? The van driver may have been taking the zombies somewhere to be dealt with safely, but he may also have been a part of something sinister. There was no way to get answers.

But I have a phone. I can get help.

Realising she had time and safety, Laura lifted the phone and pressed a button. The dim glow extinguished the surrounding darkness and allowed her to see. Various equipment, perhaps of a medical nature, cluttered the ground around her feet. She spotted an aluminium flask and a pair of thick rubber gloves, and it only gave her more questions. When she pressed numbers on the phone, nothing came up on the screen. It was only a soft beeping that told her that her inputs even registered. She hit a button marked MENU and that brought up an option for CONTACTS. She entered a sub-menu and found a single number listed as UNNAMED.

The van driver said there was only one number.

It doesn't even look like a proper number. It starts with three zeroes.

I have to call it. It's our only chance. Rose is out there without me. Danny is sick. Conner is just a boy. This needs to be me.

Laura pressed the call button and lifted the phone to her ear. She waited for a dial tone but heard only a series of clicks and buzzes. Then the noise ended and there was nothing but silence.

Is someone there? Is that breathing I hear?

"Hello? Hello, is anybody there?" No answer. "I need help. There was a crash and the driver of a white van had this phone on him. We need help."

Silence.

"Please."

"Who is this?"

"M-My name is... Sarah." Laura didn't know why she chose to lie, but the other voice had not seemed kind. "S-Sarah Thomas. I was with my friends, driving, and we came upon a car crash. We stopped to help, but people are hurt. There were two people locked inside the back of the van. There's something wrong with them. Please, can you—"

"Where are you?"

"I... I don't know. On a back road in Devon, heading for the motorway. Can't you trace the call? Are you the police?"

"How many of you are there?"

She lied again, wanting to feel safer by imagining a large number of people with her. "Ten. It was a bad crash. Please, send help."

"Stay exactly where you are. Help is coming."

The line went dead. A flood of relief washed over Laura, but it was murky. The police wouldn't have put down the phone on her. Nor would they have answered the call so abruptly. She had spoken to someone else. The van driver's employer, perhaps?

Someone's on their way. But who?

I need to know what's going on. I need to know who the van driver was working for.

He's still out there, crawling around blindly in the grass. Does he have a wallet on him? Paperwork? What if there's paperwork in here? I need to look around.

Laura got down onto her knees and pawed through the

various debris. She tried to examine each item in the glow of the phone's tiny screen, but found most to be either foreign or mundane. At one point, she almost cut herself on a broken test tube, and she then hurt her ankle by leaning on something angular and hard. When she eventually reached the cage at the back, she ran her hands carefully over the floor and walls. The wall to her left was slippery, and her hand came back caked in blood. Before the van had flipped over, it would have been the floor, which led Laura to realise that her hand was soaked in the blood of the two dead people who had been locked inside the cage. Disgusted, she wiped her hand on her bare stomach. She was feeling the cold, but as there was nothing she could do about it she pushed it to the back of her mind and tried not to let it distract her.

Finally, she found something of interest. Her hair brushed against something protruding from the ceiling near the back of the van. She lifted the phone and illuminated a small cabinet bolted to the side wall. A drawer filled the top third, and when she yanked it open, loose papers fell free and fluttered around her head. She scrambled to pick them up, and once she had gathered them all, she read the top page in the glow from the phone. It was some kind of delivery receipt.

Secure Handover Manifest: Arrangement Date: 9.10.2021 / 0200hrs

CARGO: SUBJECTS ZED AND ELIZA (Hazardous. Infectious.)

DELIVERY: Englewulf Marina, Red Hollow (The *Clarence Bounty*)

CLEARANCE PHRASE: See Daily Codex – Section 9, Quadrant 3

CONDUCT LEVEL: 6

Laura didn't know exactly what she was looking at, but it clearly wasn't good. The dead had been caged in the back of this van like livestock. Had they been bound for a boat? The *Clarence Bounty*? She knew Red Hollow was a town near Bristol, so that added up. The mention of clearance phrases and conduct levels made her think of spies and trained killers. None of it filled her with hope.

Don't let your mind wander.

She searched for a logo on the piece of paper, or some other identifying mark that might tell her who was behind all of this, but all she could find was a tiny black-and-white image in the top left corner. Two large-finned fish chasing each other in a circle. It didn't exactly cry *evil*.

She checked the other pages, and they made even less sense, although she kept spotting that same fish symbol. One sheet appeared to be some kind of scientific document, full of jargon and chemical symbols. Another was a list of names under the heading: Z SPHERE AGENTS. Several names had been crossed out in pen.

Looks like a hit list.

No, it's just a list of names. Nothing more. It's probably an employee roster.

What the hell is a Z Sphere agent?

Laura folded the papers and put them in the back pocket of her jeans. Suddenly, she felt more in danger than ever, not just from the zombies outside, but from whatever organisation the two black fish represented.

The organisation I just called on this weird phone.

What have I done?

To make matters worse, Laura detected a familiar, horrifying sound. Rose was crying. Loudly. In fact, she was wailing out for her mummy. The banging fists against the van's rear doors abruptly ceased.

The dead moved away, their moans growing distant.

They're after my baby.

Laura heard something else: the faint, almost undetectable sound of singing. It was 'Let it Go' from *Frozen.*

Conner's singing to her. He's trying to calm her down.

It's not working. I need to get out of here. I need to do something.

Mummy's coming, baby-girl.

Chapter Eleven

"Mummy's coming." Laura hurried up the stairs to fetch Rose from her nap. Her dozy cries had come through the baby monitor five minutes ago, and she was now fully awake. Nap time was infrequent now, but it seemed like only yesterday that Rose had been a tiny baby snoozing in her cot. Now, she was almost three.

It's all happening so fast. Life.

"Will you hurry up and get her?" Danny shouted from the living room. "I can't stand her crying."

"I'm on my way, aren't I?" Laura took the stairs two steps at a time. Danny had been in a foul mood all day, and her only mercy was that he hadn't got out of bed until eleven. This pandemic was going to be the death of them. Without a job, Danny had grown irritable and lazy, only moving from the bed to the sofa and back again. For the first two weeks of the national lockdown, he had seemed to enjoy his time at home with Laura and Rose, but lately he acted like they were a constant pain in his arse.

It's not like he even does anything with us. He hasn't

played with Rose in days, and I do my best to stay out of his way most of the time. Rose and I went on a walk for two hours this morning just to give him some peace, and he's still moody.

Getting paid not to work sounded great, but the reality was very different. Being at home all the time was clearly unhealthy, and Laura lived under a constant cloud of gloom and anxiety. Danny could yell at her at any moment, and nothing seemed to make him happy. Where was the sweet, affectionate man she had married?

He's always been grumpy. He's always liked things a certain way. It's only got difficult because we're stuck at home together twenty-four hours a day. I bet every couple is struggling like us.

Rose was sitting up on her bed when Laura entered her tiny bedroom. When she saw her mummy, she reached out with both arms to be scooped up. Laura kissed her on both chubby cheeks, and their identical red hair tangled together.

"Did you have a nice nap, honey?"

"Yes, Mummy. Did you?"

Laura chuckled. "Mummy didn't have a nap. I've been cleaning the kitchen. Shall we go have some lunch? How does fish fingers sound?"

"Yummy."

"Let's go, then."

"Bunny!"

"Oh, yes. We can't forget bunny." Laura reached down and grabbed her daughter's fluffy pink bunny and gave it to her. Then, smiling, she carried her daughter down the stairs and set her down at the bottom.

When Rose saw Danny sitting on the sofa, she ran excitedly towards him. "Daddy."

Danny's face was impassive, but he scooped Rose up

dutifully and gave her a cuddle. "Hey, rosebud. You have a nice sleep?"

"Yeah. Can we play?"

"Not now. Daddy's watching the news." Rose moaned and asked again, but Danny put her down and shook his head. "I said not now, honey. Go play with Mummy."

Laura rolled her eyes. *Yeah, sure. I'll play with her while I make lunch, tidy up, and suck your dick twice a week, shall I?*

"Are you going to take a walk today?" Laura asked him, wishing he would get some fresh air and cheer up.

He shrugged, eyes glued to the television. "What's the point?"

"It's good to stretch your legs and get out. You can take Rose."

"I can't be arsed. You take her."

"I took her out this morning. It's your turn."

He looked at her now, his blank expression turning spiteful. "My turn? Why don't you get a full-time job and then we'll talk about who does what around here?"

"You're not working at the moment, Danny."

"Is that my fault? No. And I'm still getting paid, so I'm still the one paying the bills."

Laura put out a hand to Rose and beckoned her over. She didn't like her listening when Daddy was like this. "I'm just saying I need some help around here, Danny. You can't just laze around all day while I do everything. It's ridiculous."

She went into the kitchen with Rose, handing her a pear that would occupy her until lunch was cooked. She didn't expect Danny to follow her, so it was a fright when he appeared right behind Laura with his fists clenched. He backed her up against the fridge and snarled. "Can I just have one day where you don't fucking nag me? You're doing my head in."

Laura baulked. "I'm doing *your* head in? You act like you hate me and treat me like your slave. I don't understand why you're so mad at me. What have I done?"

"I'm not mad at you." His teeth ground together. He was seething. "I'm just fed up being stuck inside this fucking house."

"Then go for a walk, get some fresh air, because I can't go on like this. I won't, Danny."

His upper lip curled. "Are you threatening to leave me? Go right ahead."

Laura felt tears coming. She wasn't usually one to cry, but lately it seemed like she was on the verge of sobbing almost constantly. "I'm not threatening to leave you, Danny. I'm just telling you to snap out of this and love us again. Rose and I miss you. Come back to us."

He took a deep breath and held it. Laura feared what he might do or say next, so it was a relief when he took a step back and sighed. When he spoke again, most of his anger had gone. "I hate this. I feel trapped, with nothing to do except sit around and think. This is a nightmare, Lor, and I need to get back to work. The firm has kept a couple of guys on through lockdown. Why not me? It's fucking unfair."

She smiled weakly. "You're new, that's all. I know you're struggling, Dan, but so am I. Can't we just stick together and try to make the best of this as a team? We won't have another opportunity like this – to spend all this time together – and Rose won't be this age forever. We should try to enjoy it."

"I know. You're right. I'm sorry and I'll try to cheer up, okay? I don't like being angry, but I need you to stop nagging me and deal with Rose, okay?"

"What? Danny, have you been listening to me at all?"

"Yes," he snapped. "I'll try to go easier on you, okay, but I need you to stop moping around the house and take care of things. That's your job."

"It is *not* my job, Danny. I'm not a servant or your maid."

He stepped up to her again. "I earn the money. You take care of the house and Rose. Is that not what we agreed when you were first pregnant?"

"Things are different now. You're not at work, are you? You're at home, so I have to work around you and try to stay out of your way. I don't get a break, Danny. Not for a minute. Meanwhile, all you do is sit around watching reruns of *Top Gear*. Why can't you just—"

She yelped as he lashed out and buried his fist against the fridge beside her head. He snarled like a wolf, his face mere inches from hers. "You think you know what hard work is? You have no fucking idea. Try sticking your arm in an overflowing cistern at seven o'clock in the morning or fixing a toilet that hasn't been cleaned in a year. You fill out paperwork at a fucking supermarket twice a week, so shut your mouth, okay? I don't want to hear another word. Just get lunch on and stay out of my way. Do you understand me, Lor? Am I making myself clear?"

She wanted to spit at him, to claw at his face and bite him, but she nodded meekly and said, "Yes, I understand." It was easier to give in. She couldn't bear an argument right now, with nowhere to escape to.

Damn this lockdown.

Danny moved away from her, once again sighing. "Look, I love you, Lor, you know that. Things will be better once everything goes back to normal, so let's just get through this as best we can. You're a good mum. Be proud."

"I am proud."

"Good," he leant forward and kissed her on the cheek. It made her recoil. "We'll stick a film on tonight, yeah? Maybe get a takeaway. Sound good?"

She swallowed the lump in her throat. "Can we have Chinese?"

"Whatever you want, ginge. We okay?"

She nodded meekly again as Danny walked away.

What the hell just happened? That wasn't Danny.

Or was it? Has he always been like this? Has he always been so angry?

Rose was standing at the side of the kitchen, clutching her stuffed pink bunny. She stared at Laura with wide eyes – innocent eyes that were about to cry.

"It's okay, sweetheart." She scooped her daughter up and cuddled her. "Mummy's okay."

Mummy is not okay. Mummy is trapped in a house with an angry monster.

Mummy is scared.

Chapter Twelve

Laura could not stand silently in the darkness while her daughter screamed outside. She could not stand by and do nothing while the dead stalked her family. She needed air, an escape to this cage she found herself in.

She opened the van's rear door and ducked underneath.

The chilly air once again bit at her naked torso, and the stench of death filled her nostrils. Adrenaline coursed through her veins, and she prayed for more. It sent away her tiredness and made her weak muscles strong.

The dead had reached the road's edge and were now heading across the grass towards the Nissan. Rose's screaming was luring them like a siren's song. Conner had stopped his singing. It obviously hadn't worked.

But thank you for trying.

Laura waved her hands above her head and yelled. Conner's two dead friends turned back to face her, but the obese woman continued towards the Nissan.

Please protect her, Conner. I don't know you, but I trust

you to keep my family safe. If Danny can't, then it needs to be you.

Laura waved her arms again. "Come on, you smelly shitheads. This way."

Conner's dead friends stumbled after her, and she moved towards the centre of the road. Once they caught up to her, she would lead them away, as far as possible, before doubling back around and returning to her family. The biggest problem was her pursuer's speed. Although the two dead young men stumbled and tripped, they were anything but slow. It would take a hasty jog to stay ahead of them – and Laura was no long-distance runner. If she ran out of puff, they would have a good chance of catching her.

Maybe it would be better to trick them somehow. Send them off in one direction while I sneak around behind them. But what if I take too long? Rose needs me right now.

Laura glanced at the Nissan and witnessed the large woman smashing her fists against the driver's side window. Her substantial bulk put a frightening amount of force behind her blows, and Laura could hear the glass rattling in its frame. Meanwhile, Conner's dead friends were now right on top of her, forcing her to dodge around and backpedal. They gave her little time to think.

She returned to Conner's car and hurried around the bonnet while waving her hands at her dead pursuers. "That's it. Follow me." She then crouched down, trying to disappear from their sight. They staggered around the car, searching for her.

I need to lead them further away than this. I need enough time to get to Rose, grab her, and get the hell out of here.

Laura crept alongside the hatchback, shouting at the dead men to follow her. They did, moaning and reaching out their arms. She was prepared to die to protect her daughter, and leading the dead away like this seemed a good plan, even if she never made it back to the Nissan. At least they would be away from Rose, and Conner would have fewer threats to deal with.

Laura heard breaking glass.

Oh no. No, no, no.

She stopped dead in her tracks, allowing the two dead men to catch up to her and almost grab her. She only just managed to duck beneath their arms, but she then sprinted back towards the Nissan with no thought of her previous plan. With only a brief head start, she would have to move fast. This was it. Now or never.

We have to get out of here.

She screamed and shouted, trying to catch the obese woman's attention. But the dead woman had already turned away from the Nissan and was wandering towards the trees. Something was luring her away; something more enticing than Rose's cries.

She's chasing someone.

Laura realised then that Conner had jumped out of the car and was leading the dead woman away. It was working, because, despite Rose's cries, the large corpse staggered hungrily after him as he back-pedalled alongside the trees. "That's it," he kept shouting. "That's it. You and I are going to take a little walk. But no holding hands, okay? I already have a girlfriend. She's an English major. Going to be a world-famous author. You can't beat that, I'm afraid."

Laura grinned, manic with relief and amused by Conner's mad ramblings, but she became confused when he suddenly turned and sprinted in her direction. "What are you doing?" she yelled.

"Laura. Catch!"

Something glinted in the darkness, arcing through the air towards her. It struck the road near her feet and skidded several feet.

"My keys," Conner shouted, trying to be heard over his own car's blaring stereo. "Hide in my car while I lead them away, then grab Danny and Rose and get the hell out of here."

"Wh-What about you?"

He jogged backwards, keeping one eye on his corpulent pursuer. "Once you get away, I'll head into the woods and climb a tree. Get help, Laura. We can't let anyone else get hurt."

Laura nodded, trying to work out if this was a trick. Surely this young man who owed her nothing was not putting himself in danger to help her family?

He is. He's a hero.

No, he's just a kid.

There was no time to think, and she couldn't reject the chance to get away, so Laura snatched Conner's car keys and sprinted to his car, throwing herself inside and closing the door just as his two dead friends made it back. Blessedly, she switched off the blaring radio and then slunk down into the footwell. Conner's shouting attracted her pursuers, so they continued on, right past Laura, and headed towards the woods.

Laura risked a glance over the windowsill as Conner led the dead away. He kept to the long grass growing alongside the road, giving himself the opportunity to dash into the trees if he needed to. All four zombies shambled after him now, moving further and further away from the Nissan and Rose.

My family is safe. Is this nightmare finally over? Maybe I can find Conner's phone in all of this gore and finally call for help. It's over.

She watched Conner lead the dead away for a moment longer, frightened to move and risk messing things up. He was almost at the furthest reaches of the Nissan's rear headlights now, about to enter the darkness. Light on his feet, he hopped and sidestepped, facing his pursuers head on as he led them away. Calm and collected. Completely in control.

Then he tripped.

At first, Laura didn't know what had happened. Then she spotted the van driver, groping blindly and half-hidden in the long grass. Conner had tripped right over him, falling to the ground.

Oh no!

The dead were on him in seconds. He tried to make it back to his feet, but the van driver caught his jean pocket and clung to him. As Conner battled to get free, his former friends fell upon him and started to eat. His screams pierced the air, pained and desperate. It was the gargling falsetto of a young, intelligent soul meeting an unexpected and premature end. A tragic symphony.

Laura wept.

You bastards. You fucking bastards.

Laura trembled, unsure of what to do. The dead had moved twenty-odd feet away from the Nissan, but it wasn't far enough. They would see her if she tried to make it back to Rose. She didn't even know what state Danny was in.

What the hell should she do? What would put an end to this terror?

Before she could get a hold of herself, the worst happened.

The dead removed themselves from Conner's lifeless body and stumbled back towards the Nissan. Rose's crying once again attracted them. Was Danny not trying to quieten her?

She needs me. My baby needs her mummy.

The dead surrounded the Nissan on both sides. Rose screamed louder.

Keep our daughter safe, Danny. Comfort her. Stop her crying.

Laura looked down and saw the car keys in her hands. Should she drive out of there and find help? Could Danny protect Rose while she was gone? What about Conner's phone? It was still lying somewhere in the driver's footwell, covered in gore.

There was no time to call for help.

There was no chance of reaching safety.

I'm the only one who can fix this.

Laura grabbed the guts-covered steering wheel. She started the engine and selected first gear. Then she put her foot down.

Mummy's coming.

Chapter Thirteen

"I mean, I get what you're saying, but is it really what you want?" Danny held her hand across the glass table, circling his thumb around her palm. He looked at her intensely, his crystal-blue eyes fixed in place. The candlelight flickered in his irises.

Laura's head was fuzzy from what might be her last glass of wine for several months. Her tummy was a cauldron, filled with a frothy mixture of emotions. Happiness fought for dominance, but it was being overpowered by the bitter tang of fear and dread. The decisions ahead of her were life-changing. "I don't know what I want, Dan. I want to be a nurse, but if we go ahead with this, then..."

Dan smiled at her, gazing at her like she was the only thing on Earth. The restaurant was full of people chatting, but their voices seemed to fade away. "You can still be a nurse. You can go back to your training in a couple of years. I mean, if you even want to by then."

"Why wouldn't I want to?"

He shrugged and let go of her hand. Leaning back in his tall-backed leather chair, he gave her a look, as if she didn't understand something obvious. "Well, do you really want to spend your life cleaning up blood and shit at all hours of the day? Being a nurse might sound good, but all the ones I've ever met are miserable. It's a shit job."

She raised an eyebrow. "How many nurses have you met, Dan?"

"I used to go out with a nurse, and I barely saw her for all the hours she worked. It might have been worth it if she was happy and rich, but she was neither. You can do better, Lor. You can do anything."

"Not if I have this baby. I'm not sure now is the right time for this."

He reached forward, took a swig from his beer, and then let out a sigh. "You want to have my kids, don't you?"

She chuckled, but suddenly she felt like she was being accused of something. "Of course, I do. I love you. I'm just not sure if—"

"If you intend to have a family with me, then why delay it? It's earlier than planned, maybe, but it is planned. Look, you can still be anything you want to be, Lor. A couple of years from now and the baby will go to nursery. I'll be making plenty of money by then, and I'm sure your dad will help us out financially until then."

"Maybe. I just—"

"This could be really great. You, me, and a baby. Maybe a little boy we can take to the park and push on the swings."

Laura nodded. It did sound lovely. Danny could be so erratic at times. A child might help him settle down and put to bed some of his insecurities. His own father had been a bully, using Danny as a punchbag—once even slicing his hand open with a broken beer bottle – before abandoning him and his mum forever. A baby would be a chance for Danny to move on from his past. Maybe he could finally let go of the anger that always seemed to bubble away inside him. Laura liked the thought of him healing.

But I'm not sure I want this baby. I was going to finish my studies and then move back home.

It's not the right time.

Danny reached forward and took her hand again. "You were made for this, Lor. You're fierce and independent and would make an amazing mum. We could have the best life ever. This baby is meant to be. We can't get rid of it. It's waiting for us to love it."

His eyes pierced into her, getting right beneath her skin. His thumb rubbed a little too firmly against her palm. The wine sat in front of her in a long-stemmed glass, now seeming like poison. She had drunk the first sips because part of her hadn't accepted that this was really real. Was she truly going to have a baby?

What other choice is there? I can't undo it. I'm pregnant. Do I really want an abortion hanging over me?

"Okay, let's have this baby."

His eyes creased at the corners. "For real?"

She nodded. "Yeah. Let's be a family."

He whooped with joy, making everyone in the restaurant look towards them, but Danny prevented an awkward scene by announcing Laura was having his baby. It quickly became a celebration, a bunch of strangers applauding Laura as if she had done something impressive.

"Miss?" Danny waved over the waitress. "Can I have another beer and, um, what do you want, Lor? A coke."

She shrugged. "I suppose it will have to be."

"Coming right up," said the waitress, scrunching up her nose and smiling at Laura. "Congratulations."

"Thanks."

Danny buzzed, grinning like a lunatic. He was already

making plans. "We need to move out of our flat, buy a house. We need a spare room. A cot..."

She couldn't help but laugh at his excitement. He was her beautiful, blue-eyed boy, and now the father of her baby. She had always dreamed of having her own family, and with a man she loved. "Don't get carried away, Dan. We'll take it one step at a time, yeah. And I'm going to hold you to your word about going back into nursing. I don't want to end up like my mum, stuck at home cleaning the house while you work."

He nodded, but she wasn't sure he heard her. "Yeah, of course, whatever you want, babe." He looked over at the next table and thanked a man who was giving him a thumbs up. She had never seen him prouder.

Laura wondered if she should be feeling proud, too, but at the moment she had too many emotions swirling around to tell how she felt. Life had changed in an instant, and it was a little terrifying.

She looked at her half-finished glass of wine and moved it away with the side of her hand. Just how many other things would she have to give up?

None of that matters.

I'm going to be a mum.

Laura looked at Danny and smiled. This would be the making of him; she was sure.

We're going to be a family.

Chapter Fourteen

Laura turned the slippery steering wheel, locking the Nissan in her sights. She shifted into second gear and stamped on the accelerator. The distance between the two vehicles was short, but time seemed to stretch on forever, allowing Laura to take in every detail through the rain-soaked windscreen. She saw dead people tormenting her family, saw their filthy clothing and their lumpy, distended flesh. She saw the evil unleashed by her irresponsible actions.

No. Not my actions. Danny's. He did this. He dragged us away from my parents' house in the middle of the night and got behind the wheel drunk. It was him who threw my phone out of the window because he didn't want me apologising for his behaviour. Danny caused all of this. Because I let him.

When did I give Danny control of my life?

Rose. I gave up everything when she was born. I feel guilty for not wanting her when Danny did, and I've been trying to make up for it every day since. He let me convince myself that I was the bad guy.

But I'm not.

Rose needs a strong, healthy, happy mother. Not... this.

We're getting out of here, baby-girl. You and me.

Somehow, Laura had thought all this in a single second, and now that her mind was clear, she closed her eyes and gripped the steering wheel. Her body bucked in the seat as Conner's car leapt off the road and into the wet, uneven grass.

There was an almighty bang as the car came to an immediate stop, and Laura was thrown forward as if shoved in the back. Her face plunged into a cloud and her world became noise. Rending metal. Car horns blaring.

Then silence.

Laura had no idea what speed she had achieved before the jarring impact, and it was impossible to see past the airbag, but she had felt and heard the damage to both cars. She just prayed Rose had still been on the far side of the Nissan, away from the impact.

She had aimed the car at the dead, but they had been spread out around the Nissan. It was impossible that she had hit them all.

But I can't hear them moaning any more.

I can't hear Rose crying either.

Oh God.

Laura knew she had to get out of the car, but she needed a second to catch her breath – a second of calm where, in her mind at least, the dead remained dead and her family were not in danger. She flexed each muscle to see if she was injured, but other than an ache in her collarbone and a banging in her head, she felt nothing. The hatchback's interior and exterior lights had all switched on, dispelling the night. There was also an insistent beeping sound. And something else...

Rose was crying.

Oh, thank God. I'm coming, honey.

Knowing she could sit in a daze no longer, Laura leant against the driver's side door and pulled on the handle. She almost fell out onto the grass, and quickly realised that her legs had turned hollow. It took several seconds of flexing and rotating her ankles before she trusted them to hold her weight. She saw no dead and still couldn't hear their moans. The air had the scent of metal, but it was mild. The rain fell incessantly, but wasn't unwelcome. It caressed Laura's naked skin as she stood there in her bra and jeans, and it made her feel alive.

Rose's cries got her moving.

She limped around to the front of the Nissan to give herself a better vantage point of the damage done. Immediately, she gasped. The obese dead woman had been sliced clean in half. Her severed torso was plonked across the hatchback's crumpled bonnet, which was wedged up against the Nissan's side. Her arms swam in her own guts as she tried to remove herself from the wreckage, but her tangled viscera held her in place. There was a second body, crushed beneath the hatchback's front wheels, but it was hard to tell who it was. The smart white trainer, still attached to a wiggling foot, suggested it was one of Conner's former friends.

I got two of them.

So where are the others?

As if to answer her question, the original zombie – the one with the badly broken arm – came rushing around from the other side of the Nissan, reaching out with his one hand and attempting to seize Laura by the neck. She dodged aside and grabbed *him* by the broken arm. The feel of blistered, weeping flesh between her fingers was vile, and her every cell recoiled, but she was done with being a frightened victim. It was time to fight back. She twisted her hips and sent the dead man crashing against the Nissan. His legs tangled, and he fell face first onto the wet grass. For good measure, she stomped on his back, planting her heel right between his shoulder blades. It might have been her imagination, but she thought she felt something crunch, and it gave her an unexpected thrill.

But it would be only moments before the dead man got back to his feet.

Feeling safer when she was moving, Laura headed around to the far side of the Nissan, watching the darkness of the woods as she passed alongside the tree line. The impact had shunted the Nissan away from the tree trunk it had been stuck up against, and it now sat in a gap between two tall trees. Its flickering headlights cast dancing shadows.

Where were the remaining dead? And was Rose hurt? To find out, she looked in through the back window.

But Rose and Danny weren't inside.

"What? No! Where are you? Where are you?"

A hissing sound above her head caused her to look up. A figure loomed over her from the roof of the car. It was Danny. He had clambered through the sunroof, with Rose held in front of him. "Lor! Lor, what happened?"

"I crashed Conner's car," she said. "I had to keep the dead from getting to you and Rose."

He nodded, an almost-smile forming on his swollen lips. "It worked. Now we need to get out of here."

It was good to see Danny alert and competent, and the impact hadn't seemed to have injured him. His wrist, however, was still a bloody mess at his side, and his face was almost unrecognisable. "Take Rose," he said, holding their daughter under the arms and moving her to the edge of the roof. She wailed and thrashed.

"Mummy! Mummy!"

"I'm here baby-girl. Come to me."

Laura reached out as Danny half lowered, half dropped Rose into her arms. She almost fell beneath the sudden extra weight, but the mania coursing through her system kept her strong. She cradled Rose against her chest, and it felt amazing. In fact, she wondered if she could ever let go. She looked up at Danny. "Now you. Come on, hurry."

The remaining dead heard the commotion and headed around the Nissan's boot. Conner's remaining friend, as well as Conner himself. Seeing the dead young man up close tore away some of Laura's anger and left sadness in its place. She had barely known the kid, but he had been brave and compassionate and smart. If they made it out of this alive, Laura would make sure people heard about his courage.

If I ever have a son, the name's already in the bag.

Danny stood at the edge of the roof. Laura waved an arm at him to hurry. "Now! Jump now."

The dead closed in. The zombie with the broken arm had made it to his feet and was navigating around the Nissan's bonnet.

Danny looked down at Conner and then looked at Laura. He was afraid. Fear was something Laura had rarely seen on her husband's face, but right now he was sick with it. He was the man she loved – emotional, sensitive, and flawed – and he was frozen in panic.

"It's okay, Danny, I'm here. We're getting out of here together. You, me, and Rose. You just need to come to me."

Danny nodded, swallowed deeply, and took a half step backwards. Then he leapt. Instead of hopping down off the roof cautiously, and risk being grabbed by the approaching dead, Danny launched himself from the edge of the roof with everything he had. He came crashing down on the grass beside Laura, but instead of landing evenly on both legs, he came down at an angle. His feet immediately slipped from beneath him and went up in the air. If not for the life-and-death situation, it might have been comical, but when he crashed down on his back, the wind escaped him in an agonised howl and left him paralysed. Laura moaned, matching her husband's anguish. With Rose in her arms, she could do little to help him, but still she did her best to reach down with one hand to help him up.

Come on, come on. Get up, Danny.

Conner and his friend attacked. Both lunged for Laura, forcing her to back up and abandon Danny. Rose was silent in her arms, perhaps sensing that her cries would do nothing to help. Laura, however, squealed in terror. As she moved towards the woods, the dead went after her, and as she exited the glow of the headlights, she found herself in complete darkness. Everywhere she turned, she came up against a tree or tripped over undergrowth. She could barely see the dead behind her, and their pale faces caught only the merest slithers of moonlight.

I won't let them get Rose.

They can go to Hell.

Laura backed up and hit another tree, unable to go in that direction. She sidestepped, trying to find space, but Conner caught up to her and grabbed her bra by the shoulder strap. She struggled, ducking and leaning to keep Rose away from his hungry mouth, but he wouldn't let go.

There was something in Conner's eyes that still seemed human, and rather than bite her, he gnashed at the air and moaned. His slick black hair spilled down the front of his face. His handsomeness was not yet fully spoiled.

"C-Conner?"

His teeth ground together in a snarl. Something like intelligence flashed in his eyes, and it appeared he might speak to her, but instead he lunged for her neck.

"Lor!" Danny barged Conner aside just as he was about to sink his teeth into Laura's neck. Her bra strap stretched and almost broke, but then the elastic whipped back and bit her naked flesh. After what she'd been through, the sudden jolt of pain barely registered. Conner stumbled backwards, staying on his feet for a moment, until a tangled bush caused him to stumble into the undergrowth.

Danny grabbed Laura and looked at her. His face was an inhuman mess of red veins and clammy grey flesh, but he spoke clearly. "I've got you, ginge. Nothing is going to hurt you or Rose. I swear it."

Laura nodded, unable to speak. Her breaths were shallow and icy. Raindrops gathered on the leaves above and merged into larger blobs that dripped more heavily. Several times, Laura got water in her eyes, but she was able to wipe her face with a forearm and keep moving. Rose buried her head against her shoulder, trembling like a leaf.

The three of them headed deeper into the woods. Conner and his friend gave chase, with the original zombie not far behind them. The three corpses moved quickly, without the human fears of tripping or colliding with trees in the dark. Laura and Danny were forced to move more cautiously, arms out in front, legs kicking forward and probing ahead. If one of them fell, it was all over. Their pursuers were quick, and they wouldn't stop.

How deep are these woods? Where do they lead? What if they go on forever?

Don't be stupid, Lor. Nothing goes on forever. Everything has an end. There's probably a housing estate right on the other side of these trees. This is England, not the Congo.

They hurried, moving deeper and deeper into the dark nothingness. Twigs and leaves crunched underfoot. Rain battered the branches overhead. The dead moaned hungrily behind them.

But they were okay. For now, she, Rose, and Danny were okay. They were racing for their lives, but it felt better than hiding and cowering. No longer trapped prey.

Just hunted prey now.

Laura collided with a tree, smashing her elbow and summoning a flash of white-hot pain. She yelled in agony, and Danny grabbed her to keep her moving. He said something to her, but it came out as an incomprehensible gurgle. When she glanced sidewards at him, as they passed through a patch of moonlit scrub, she noticed he was drooling – a mixture of blood and saliva. He was dying. She knew it. Every second that passed took him further away from life and closer to whatever came next. How much longer did he have before he dropped?

They needed to get to safety before it was too late. Danny needed urgent medical attention.

Fuck, we need the goddamn army.

Up ahead, the darkness of the forest turned grey as the moonlight found more openings in the canopy. The tall trees thinned out, and the ground was clear of brush. This might be the end of the woods, but what would they find on the other side? An empty field? Another road? Laura knew her hopes of finding people were probably naïve. A miracle would not come true – they were in the middle of nowhere. She just hoped for... *something*.

Danny tripped onto his knees, and Laura slowed to help him. He waved her away. "No. Go. Go!"

But Laura couldn't. She went back and grabbed Danny's arm, helping him to get to his feet. The dead were only several steps behind, bouncing off the trees like pinballs. Somehow they used their clumsiness to add to their momentum. It was impossible to outrun them while dealing with an injured Danny and an increasingly heavy Rose. They couldn't keep running. They needed to hide again.

Or fight back.

"I think... I think the woods are ending." Laura was sure they were about to break free of the trees, and it filled her with trepidation. The moonlight grew brighter, and fewer and fewer trees got in her way. She picked up her pace, less fearful of tripping or running into obstacles. It allowed Laura to put a little more distance between her and the dead.

Danny also fell behind.

Laura pumped her legs, trying to ignore the increasing heaviness of her thighs. She reached the last of the trees and burst out into an open – empty – field. It was just as she had feared. She couldn't keep running with Rose in her arms. The dead would outlast her.

But then she saw something to her left that offered hope. A building. The silhouette of a farmhouse or a cottage, rounded edges suggesting a thatched roof rather than tiled. Various other shapes dotted the landscape, too, and Laura quickly made out tractors, trailers, and other farming equipment. Her ears detected the gentle mooing of cows, and there was an angular shadow that might have been a barn.

They had found salvation. It was a house, and houses meant people, phones, solid doors, and sharp weapons. Laura glanced back and was dismayed to see that Danny had fallen behind. He was closer to the dead than he was to Laura and Rose.

"Danny! Please, keep going. We're almost there. I just need you to go a little while longer. Come to me."

He didn't respond, but he picked up speed, edging away from the dead and towards the living. Laura slowed her pace so he could catch up to her, but once he had, she broke into a full-on sprint and hoped he could keep up. He did, moaning and wheezing the whole time, but managing to stay on her heels. He sounded like an old man, not her strong, confident Danny at all.

Just keep going, Danny. Keep on running.

And he did. He ran and he ran, and he didn't give up. He stayed with Laura and Rose.

Laura loved him for that.

With her destination in sight, Laura put every shred of energy she had left into her run. A stitch threatened to tear her in two, but she ignored it. She had to reach the farmhouse, and quickly enough to bang on the door and wait for the startled inhabitants to get out of bed and let them in.

What if there's no one home, or they don't open up?

Time to stop imagining the worse, Lor. It's already happened and you're still kicking.

In the near darkness, Laura almost collided with a low stone wall. She half skidded, and awkwardly hopped just in time to leap over it. Being a few steps behind, Danny had enough warning to see it early and leap it in his stride. He wheezed heavily but showed no signs of stopping.

Debris littered the yard in front of the farmhouse, forcing Laura to slow down and watch her step. Old oil drums and car parts sat in a pile next to some kind of attachment for a tractor. She feared the place was derelict but then heard the cattle mooing again inside the nearby barn. There was also a light on in one of the building's upstairs rooms. Somebody definitely lived here.

This is our chance. This all ends now.

Laura looked back, glad to see the dead struggling with the low stone wall. It would be several moments before they got themselves over it. Danny was with her. Rose was alive in her arms. They were together.

"Mummy's got you," Laura whispered in her daughter's ear. "Mummy will take care of everything." She hurried up to the front door, hand raised in a fist.

The door opened before she had time to knock on it.

Two dark eyes appeared in front of her. The man behind them was old and angry. "You came to the wrong house," he said. "The wrong goddamn house."

Chapter Fifteen

"Please," said Laura. "Please, we need help."

An old man, dressed in slippers and pyjamas, scowled at her from behind a long twin-barrelled shotgun. Slowly his eyes moved from Laura's pleading face down to Rose, who was trembling in her arms. "Who are you people? Why are you half-naked? Speak."

"There's no time to explain."

"Then make time."

Danny shambled to a stop beside Laura and mumbled something incoherent. It seemed to take effort even for him to stand, so she pressed up against him, trying to take some of his weight.

The old man studied Danny, bulbous red nose wrinkling in disgust. "The hell is wrong with him? He looks about ready to drop dead."

Laura glanced over her shoulder. The three dead men were past the low stone wall and were now shambling eagerly towards the farmhouse. She turned back to face the old man, her grip on Rose loosening as her arms turned numb. "There's no time to explain, so please let us in. The people behind us are dangerous. We need your help."

The shotgun pointed at Laura's face began to tremble and the old man seemed suddenly unsure. "What trouble have you brought to my doorstep? I'm not getting involved in someone else's mess."

Danny mumbled, managing to form words. "Please. My wife. My daughter. Help... them."

The shotgun continued to tremble in the old man's hands, and for a moment, Laura was unsure if he would just pull the trigger and ask questions later. Thankfully, with an irritated sigh he lowered the shotgun, and then stood aside for them to enter. "Inside," he barked. "Quickly. And wipe your feet."

Laura nodded and thanked him profusely, but she also warned him. "You can't let those men inside. They're dangerous."

"I'll handle it."

Laura, Rose, and Danny shuffled across a balding coir matt and then stepped onto a tiled floor. They found themselves inside a cluttered sitting room with an old-fashioned fireplace and a flowery three-settee arrangement in the middle of a giant brown rug. A pair of dull lamps currently lit the room, but large windows on three of the four walls would probably let in a great deal of sunlight by day.

Laura placed Rose down on the largest of the three settees and grabbed an old-fashioned knitted blanket that was folded over the armrest. "Stay here, honey. Keep yourself warm."

"Want my bunny. Mummy, I want my bunny."

Laura felt a stab in her heart. She stroked her daughter's silky red hair and fought back tears. "I know you do, honey. I'll get your bunny as soon as I can, I promise."

"Want to go home."

"We'll be home soon, honey, I promise."

"I want to go home now!"

"Rose, please..."

The old man had remained in the doorway, staring out into the darkness with his shotgun. The open door let in the cold. "Whoever you are," he yelled. "You need to get off my property, right now. If you don't, I'll feed you to my pigs."

Laura moaned. "Close the door. You can't hurt them."

"Like hell I can't."

"If you shoot them, they'll just keep on coming."

"Sh-She's right," said Danny, slumping down on a wooden chair set against the wall.

The old man glanced back at them like they were mad. He kept his shotgun pointed out of the door. "They on drugs? Are you?" He eyed Laura in her bra. "Looks like you've escaped an orgy."

"Just close the door," said Danny, voice thick like he had the flu. "W-We'll tell you everything, but close... the... the door."

"Please," begged Laura, clutching herself to try and keep out the cold. "You have to listen to us."

The old man was clearly unhappy about it, but he grabbed the front door by its edge and slammed it shut. It rattled loosely in its frame. Then, the old man propped his shotgun up against a wooden bureau and bolted the door, top and bottom. Turning back to face the room, he tutted. "You'd better have a good story to tell, because I'm far too old and far too short of patience for this nonsense."

"We need to be quiet," said Laura. "If we're quiet, they might go away." It had worked in the car, so why wouldn't it work now? The room's windows were all covered by curtains, so they only needed to remain silent. For now, however, the dead knew they were inside. They crashed up against the other side of the front door and started battering it with their fists, moaning hungrily with the desire for human flesh.

The old man reached for his shotgun. "Bloody fools."

Laura begged him again. "Don't open the door."

"I can handle this," he said, anger in his voice. "I'm not having it."

"They're dead," she said, not knowing how else to convince him. "I can't explain it, but the people outside are dead. Please, just call the police. Let them handle it."

For several seconds, the old man just stared at her. Then he shook his head in dismay. "You're right. I'm going to call the police and let them deal with this nonsense." He put down his shotgun and marched across the room, yanking a cream-coloured handset from the middle shelf of an old-fashioned china cabinet. He placed the receiver to his ear and dialled 999 on the keypad. He quickly placed it down again. "It's dead."

"Dead?" said Danny, still slurring. "You're... sure?"

"Yes, I'm sure. There's no dial tone."

"Do you have a mobile phone?" asked Laura.

"Of course I do. Reception's no good out here, but I keep one around for emergencies."

"Well, this *is* an emergency."

"Yes, yes, okay. Hold on." He searched several drawers in the living room, huffing to himself the entire time. After a moment of fruitless searching, he shuffled out of the room. Several minutes later, he returned, simply saying, "Junk drawer," before showing them an old slide phone. "See? Told you I had one."

"Great," said Laura. "Call for help."

The old man squinted at the keypad and then thumbed

a button to switch it on. "Right," he said. "Here we go. Nine, nine, nine."

Laura, sitting on the sofa with Rose, glanced at Danny, who had slumped down even further on the wooden chair at the side of the room. He was drooling, and he blinked slowly, staring into space. The dash to the farmhouse had taken a lot from him. Every second, he seemed to fade more. She called out to him, concerned. "Dan?" He didn't seem to hear her, so she called out to him again. "Dan? Dan, do you need a drink of water? Come on, stay with me. Dan? Dan?"

Slowly, he turned his head in her direction. "Huh?"

"Can I get you some water? Anything?"

"Water..."

Laura ran her hand along Rose's cheek, and then knelt beside the sofa so that she could kiss it. "Would you like some water, too, honey?"

"Juice." She leant against Laura's bare arm and yawned. "And toast."

Laura chuckled. "I'll get you some water. Then we'll see if we can get something to eat. Wait right here, okay? You won't move, will you?"

"Want to go home." She pulled an angry face. Tantrums were unlike Rose, but she was clearly building towards one. Who could blame her?

Laura stood up and moved away from the sofa.

The old man spoke loudly into his ancient mobile phone, demanding the police. He'd got through to someone, but the line must have been bad because he kept closing his eyes and tilting his head to hear better. His hand shook as he held the phone, and there was a tremor in his voice. He was clearly a tough old man, but he was still an *old* man. They had turned up on his doorstep an hour before dawn, screaming and shouting about the dead walking, and those dead were now banging on his front door, hungry for flesh. He must be terrified.

But there's nothing I can do about it. He needs to keep that door closed and trust us.

Or else we're all dead.

Laura snuck by her distracted host and headed uninvited into a country-style kitchen with real wood counters and hardwood shaker doors. It was a dim and dingy room, about thirty years out of date, but it had a solid, lived-in feel to it. The entire house did.

Laura took a moment to rub at herself, trying to warm up her cold, exposed skin. She then rooted around the kitchen's wall cabinets until she found cups, and then filled one beneath a wobbly steel tap hanging over a chunky Belfast sink. The water gushed out faster than expected, and it splashed her naked stomach, making her shudder. "That's some nice pressure you've got there," she muttered, before hurrying back into the living room.

There, she found the old man still barking into the phone. It sounded like he was giving an address, which was good. She imagined the police surrounding the farmhouse and handcuffing the dead, treating them like a bunch of homeless drunks. That would be fine by her. Whatever got her, Rose, and Danny out of there in one piece.

And Danny to a hospital.

Then she thought about who she had spoken to on the van driver's phone. Were they still on their way? If so, what was taking them so long?

Rose lay on her side, sucking her thumb and snuggling against the knitted blanket. Usually, she would suck one of her bunny's ears, and the stuffed toy's absence once again stabbed at Laura's heart. It was a simple yet vitally important thing that she could not provide for her daughter. She would do anything to conjure the bunny into her hands, to make the situation just a little easier for Rose.

I've let her down. I've put her in danger.

Will she ever be able to forget this? Or have I broken a part of her forever?

Danny had stood up since Laura had left to go into the kitchen. He was now facing the front door with his back to the room. She approached him carefully, not wanting to startle him. "Dan? I have some water here for you. Are you okay?"

He started to turn slowly, his wounded wrist hanging limply by his side. It leaked like a tap, murky fluid running down his fingertips and dripping onto the tiles. A dark, lumpy puddle collected at his feet.

"D-Danny?"

He turned to face her with milky, vacant eyes. His mouth drooped to one side, the muscles gone lax. Nothing in his expression resembled the man she had married. Rather than respond to her voice, he just stood there, staring hollowly.

The old man moved up beside Laura. He had put down the phone, the call ended, and now sounded a little calmer. "Police are on their way." He said it loudly, as if he hoped the ghouls outside would hear. With nothing to distract them away from the door, they had failed to go away. "Ambulance, too," he said more quietly to Laura. "Ten minutes, they said. The line got cut off, but I told them the address first. Help is coming."

Laura was barely listening. Her eyes were fixated on Danny. He stared back at her, slack-jawed and unsteady on his feet. "Danny?" she said desperately. "Say something, please. Speak to me."

The old man set his eyes on Danny and gasped. "Jesus

wept. I've seen slaughtered pigs in better shape. Sit yourself down, son. Come on now. Just ignore those fools outside and take it easy. Easy does it..." He reached out a hand to Danny and stepped forward to help.

Danny lurched and grabbed the old man around the neck. By now, Laura's nerves had been frayed to nubs, but it allowed her to act quickly. She grabbed Danny around the waist before he could bite the old man, and pulled him away with all the strength she could muster. The old man – shocked and then angry – shoved Danny away with both hands, sending him crashing into the front door hard enough that the ageing wooden frame cracked. Danny rolled along the wall to keep his balance, leaving bloody drool marks against the grubby white paintwork.

Rose cried out from the sofa. "Daddy!"

The old man grabbed his shotgun from the bureau and wasted no time in aiming it. Laura leapt in front of him, closing her eyes and praying he didn't pull the trigger. He didn't. Instead, he cursed at her to get out of the way. "Please," she begged him. "Don't shoot. Don't shoot my husband."

"He's delirious. Get out of the way."

"Don't shoot him."

"I don't intend on shooting anyone," he grunted, "unless I have to."

Laura backed away, trusting the man to have mercy.

Danny turned back to face them. His lower lip had burst and blood was now leaking down his chin. A low rumble escaped his chest. A hungry moan.

"Stay back, Danny. Please, don't do this."

He took a clumsy step forward.

The old man raised his shotgun. "Don't push it, son."

"Danny," said Laura. "Please."

Danny shuffled forward. Blood poured from his mouth. Even more poured from his wrist.

"Daddy!" Rose sprang off the sofa, shedding the knitted blanket, and sprinted towards Danny, arms stretched out in front of her. "Daddy, you're bleeding."

Laura snatched at her daughter, trying to stop her, but she missed, grabbing empty air. It left her off balance and stumbling sidewards. "Rose! Stop!"

But she didn't stop. She raced towards her father, clearly dismayed by the sight of his bleeding arm and ruined mouth. Danny moaned, ready to embrace her with his strong arms.

"Keep away, little'un." The old man, shotgun buried in his armpit, grabbed Rose and bundled her away from Danny just in time to keep him from snatching her. His blood-soaked hands grasped at nothing.

Laura howled in a mixture of horror and relief. She took Rose by the hand and pulled her away from the thing that was no longer her father. The old man got in front of them both and nudged them towards the centre of the sitting room. He raised his shotgun and yelled a warning. "Listen, son. You're clearly unwell, so I'm not holding anything against you, but if you don't back off, I'll put a hole in your chest. I've got no reason not to." He glanced back at Laura, perhaps checking her reaction to the statement. She said nothing. Even if she wanted to beg for Danny's life, it was too late. He couldn't possibly recover from this.

I love him. He's Rose's father. But he's dangerous, and I won't let him hurt me or Rose.

The old man stood firm with his shotgun, but Danny didn't heed the warning. He staggered forward, broken teeth chomping at the air. His wrist oozed rancid filth all over the white rug. Behind him, the front door's wooden frame cracked and rattled. The dead outside were excited by all the yelling.

"I won't warn you again," said the old man. "This is it. Your last chance. Stop!"

But Danny didn't.

So the old man pulled the trigger.

The blast was the loudest thing Laura had ever heard. It caused her and Rose to squeal in dismay. The sound was so disorientating that it made it hard even to see, and several seconds went by before Laura could focus again. Then she was horrified.

Danny had stumbled backwards, right across the room. His jumper had torn open in the middle, its blackened edges smoking, and a deep hole above his belly button spilled out deep red chunks of flesh. Entrails dangled over his belt. Yet, somehow, he remained standing.

"What the hell?" The old man's voice was a wispy, faraway breeze, as if the shotgun blast had somehow struck him instead of Danny. "It-It's not possible."

Danny staggered forward again, dodging around the settees and crossing the giant brown rug even faster than before. The old man shouldered his shotgun and fired again.

Laura squealed and covered Rose's eyes.

Danny's face disintegrated from the nose down. One second he was a distorted version of her husband, the next he was a mutilated ghoul from her nightmares. His lower jaw had disappeared, exposing the remnants of a throat and the knuckles of his spine, while his once shapely nose now hung in thin air with no upper lip to support it. Blood spattered his milky grey eyes. He hadn't blinked, the simplest of human instincts no longer present.

But still he remained on his feet.

The old man dropped the shotgun and shuddered. "This is the devil's work."

"No," said Laura. "We don't need the devil's help to do bad things. Please, don't go crazy on me. Stay with me, okay?"

"Mitch."

"What?"

"M-My name. It's Mitch. You weren't lying, were you? The dead are rising."

"I'm sorry. I brought this to your doorstep, Mitch, but I need your help. We need to hide until the police get here. I need to keep my daughter safe."

Mitch stared at Danny, unable to look away. "How is this possible?"

"I don't know, but my husband, and the monsters outside, won't stop until they tear us apart. Where can we hide, Mitch? Come on!"

He glanced back at her, eyes wide, skin beneath his neck bulging. "Upstairs. We need to go upstairs."

"Then let's go."

He nodded and lead the way. Danny stumbled after them.

The front door frame cracked and splintered.

Rose called out for her daddy.

Chapter Sixteen

Laura's father eyed his cards. The whiskey on the table in front of him was almost empty, and he eyed it until Laura's mother got the hint to go and refill it. "I'll see you and raise you," he said, tapping his fanned-out cards against his chest. "I'm feeling lucky."

Danny sniffed. Then, after a moment's thought, he continued with the hand. Laura knew he hated poker – most games in fact – so it was lovely to see him make an effort, although she had needed to manage him carefully throughout the day, checking in regularly to make sure he was okay. It took very little to upset Danny when he was out of his comfort zone, and he only truly relaxed when he was at home with Laura and Rose. This weekend meant a lot to Laura, but Danny had agreed to come only reluctantly.

But at least he agreed. I'm grateful for that.

After a year of stifling lockdowns and sapping furlough schemes, it was amazing to be away from home for an entire night. Even the long journey from the Midlands down to the south coast had been wonderful, and Laura had opened the window to suck in the fresh air as if it were a rare luxury. The best thing of all, however, was watching Rose play and chitchat with Nanny and Grandad. The lockdowns had been hard on her, too. She had barely spent a month in nursery during the last year, and the only interaction she had away from home was with the random strangers who made a fuss of her at the park. Rose had needed this weekend as much as Laura. Three-year-olds weren't supposed to be cooped up inside for months at a time.

I worry how much this past year has damaged her. Will it stunt her emotional development?

No. She's a good kid, a happy kid. She'll put all this behind her. Now that the lockdowns have ended, things will go right back to normal.

It was eleven o'clock at night. Laura had put Rose down to bed an hour ago, her daughter already halfway to sleepy town. Before saying goodnight, Rose had said that the plush double bed in the guest bedroom had made her feel like a princess. Laura said that she *was* a princess, and that she should dream a wonderful dream of palaces and ponies.

Tonight had been a good night. It felt like an end to the horrors of Covid. Laura had almost forgotten that she and Danny could be happy, but tonight they had laughed and joked together just like old times.

But it had been touch and go. Things had nearly gone badly.

Don't think about it. It doesn't matter. Danny got over it. He's smiling.

They had arrived at Laura's parents' house shortly after lunchtime, and Danny had immediately turned up his nose at the food, which, to be fair, she only half blamed him for. Mussels were an acquired taste, and not something that everyone knew how to eat. Laura had needed to show

Danny what to do, and it hadn't gone down well. Her father's chuckles didn't make it any better either.

The next incident occurred shortly after they'd gone up to Laura's childhood bedroom to change their clothes and freshen up. Danny had begun rooting around her cupboards and drawers, feigning curiosity, but really he was snooping. He was trying to find a reason to get upset, which was something he did often, like he couldn't relax unless he knew exactly what to expect and what he might find.

When Danny had found a box of faded photographs buried in Laura's old dresser, a reason to be angry presented itself. One of the photographs pictured a teenaged Laura sitting on the lap of an old boyfriend, grinning away happily. It had been taken so long ago that it took her several seconds to even remember the boy's name, yet Danny had turned red in the face, trembling and frantic. His jealously was an untamed beast, and as much as he fought it, it always won. At its mercy, he would either brood silently for hours, or he would abandon all reason and yell at her. This time he chose the latter, although he tried to keep his voice down so her parents wouldn't hear. They were downstairs, watching television with Rose.

The argument was oddly surreal. She was standing there, inside the cocoon of her childhood bedroom, but was being shouted at by a fully grown man for things she had done more than a decade ago. She kept on apologising, which also felt odd, for she didn't think she had done anything wrong, but Danny wouldn't listen. The lad in the picture had been her boyfriend years before she had ever met Danny, yet he acted as though she should have been able to tell the future back then and know that she had been destined to be with him – and only him. None of this was shocking, and that might have been the worst part of it. This was an aspect of Danny that Laura knew well, and over the years she had grown wearily accepting of it. He couldn't help his insecurities – it wasn't his fault – so it was best to just grin and bear it until he calmed down. At least then he would be pleasant for a while as he sought to make up with her.

"I wish I had never been with anyone but you, Danny. Peter meant nothing to me. I was just a kid."

"Did you have sex with him?"

"What?" She really didn't want to answer that, but she knew he wouldn't let it go. "I-I don't even remember. Probably not."

"Oh my God. You did! I can see it in your face. For fuck's sake, Lor."

"I said I don't remember."

"How old were you?"

She shrugged, growing numb. "I dunno. Sixteen, seventeen. Maybe older."

"Sixteen? Fucking hell. I can't believe you were having sex at sixteen. I never realised..."

A spark of anger emerged from her, but it didn't feel wrong. "You never realised what? Anyway, how old were you?"

"This isn't about me, Lor. I'm not the one keeping old pictures of my exes around. Why do you still have it? Do you fantasise about him or something?"

"What? Danny, those photos have been buried in my dresser for years. I moved out of here when I was eighteen. If they were important to me, I would have taken them with me, wouldn't I?"

"Fine. Then I'm throwing them away."

You have no right to do that. I honestly don't care about the photos, but they're mine. They're just snaps of old friends, but it's my past. My *past, not yours. You have no right to throw my memories away.*

She sighed. "Fine. Chuck them in the bin. I don't care."

And he did. But not before tearing them into shreds and spitting on them. He even got upset about a picture of her where she was sitting alone, doing nothing but smiling. Her legs were on display.

The entire ordeal had left her feeling sick, shaken and vulnerable.

Danny had eventually calmed down and apologised, but then he had asked her to sympathise with him because of how upset he was. He just loved her so much that it hurt him to think of her with anybody else, that was all. He said it as if she should somehow be grateful, so she had held him for twenty minutes, trying to reassure him while at the same time wondering how he had somehow ended up the victim. She didn't even understand why there had to *be* a victim. Why couldn't they just have a nice time? Why was happiness so unsustainable for him? Danny was incapable of just sitting back and letting life happen.

Rose had eventually rescued Laura and Danny by begging for a bath. They had laughed along with her while she splashed in Laura's parent's jacuzzi and made bubbles. With a glass of Pinot in hand, things suddenly seemed a little less serious, so Laura had decided to let it all go. She didn't want to spoil the rest of the evening.

Dinner to follow was pleasant – roast beef and potatoes – and the continued drinking settled their nerves even further. Now, it was an hour from midnight, and they were two hours into a game of cards. Danny, despite his lack of experience at poker, was winning.

Until he wasn't.

After bluffing Danny into betting most of his chips,

Laura's dad laid down four of a kind to Danny's straight. It was an impressive end to a tense hand, but Laura saw the glint of anger flash through her husband's expression. Danny hated losing, and losing to her dad would be even worse. She suspected her dad had played her husband for a fool by allowing him several easy victories to keep the game lively, and then ending the night with a big win to take it all back. They had been playing for pennies. It meant nothing at all. Yet all the air seemed to leave the room as they sat inside the glass-fronted orangery that looked over the floodlit lawns.

Danny fell silent, downing half his beer in one sip.

Laura's father sipped his whiskey. The corners of his mouth turned upwards.

"Good game," said Laura, and she chuckled, trying to play it all off as a bit of fun – because that's what it was supposed to be. "Danny, are you going to get your revenge?"

"No. I think I'm done. Poker never was my game, anyway."

"Nonsense," said her dad, leaning back in his chair and stretching. "You've wiped the floor with me most of tonight, and you completely thrashed me the last time we played."

Danny frowned. "Last time? I don't think I've ever played poker with you before, Keith."

"Yes, you have. I remember it well. I had to teach you the rules because you had never played poker before. You kept getting it confused with blackjack, but once you got the gist, you played a blinder. Impressed us all, you did. It was a while ago, but you must remember."

Danny shook his head. "I have no idea what you're talking about."

A knot formed in Laura's stomach as a vague memory taunted her. She glared at her father, willing him to stop talking. But he didn't. He sat jerked forward in his chair and clicked his fingers. "Oh, I remember now. Sorry, Dan, I'm thinking of Peter. That's right, isn't it, Laura? He stayed over a couple of times when you used to go out. Nice chap. I wonder what happened to him."

Laura's mum spoke up—"Keith, come on," —but her meek voice went ignored.

Laura groaned. Peter was the boy in the photograph. It was probably a coincidence her father had brought him up, but it was the worst thing he could have said. "It was over ten years ago, Dad. What are you talking about?"

"Not that long ago, was it, sweetheart? What were you when you broke up – nineteen, twenty?"

"I don't know. It was a long time ago, and I was just a kid. Shut up."

Her father feigned injury. "All right, all right. Didn't mean to put my foot in it."

Danny was staring at her. He was trying to appear easy-going, but she could read him like a book. A pressure valve had just burst in his head, and it was now letting off a high-pitched screech. "You said you were sixteen when you went out with him?" he said. "You were together for four years?"

She shrugged. "It wasn't that long at all."

"He stayed over? Here?"

Laura's dad leant forward. "Come on now, Dan. Like Laura said, it was a long time ago. I didn't mean to bring up a touchy subject."

Danny pressed his lips together and then tutted. "It's fine. It's just that Laura told me something different. Whatever, though, right? We all have a past. It doesn't matter."

"Exactly. Now, are you sure you don't want to play another hand to win your pennies back?"

Danny stood up, pushing back his chair. "No, I'm tired,

Keith. I'm just going to go the toilet, and then I'll head up to bed."

Laura reached out to grab his hand, but he dodged her. She smiled at him, trying to pretend she couldn't see how angry he was. "Um, is it okay if I stay up for a little bit? I'm not tired."

He looked at her, returning a smile that didn't reach his eyes.

"Of course it's okay," her dad said. "I haven't seen my Lori-Loo for a whole year. Dan won't mind if you have a late one with your old dad, will you?"

Her mum spoke up again. "Keith..."

Danny kept his focus on Laura, breathing in and out through his nose like a snorting bull. With that false smile, he said, "Of course not, Keith. I'll just go to the toilet. Then I'll say goodnight."

But when Danny returned, he had received an unexpected text from his boss. There was an emergency job first thing in the morning – all hands on deck. They had to leave right now and go back home. Laura groaned at the ridiculousness of it. Couldn't he have come up with something better than having to go to work unexpectedly on a Sunday morning? Whose boss texted them at half eleven on a Saturday night?

Yet, despite the absurdity of the excuse, Laura's father stood up and nodded. "Of course. I understand, Dan. If you have to work, you have to work. Got to pay those bills, right?" Laura wondered if that was a dig about them sometimes asking for money to pay the mortgage, or if her dad was being genuinely understanding. It was hard to tell. As with poker, he played his cards close to his chest.

"Yep," said Danny, barely acknowledging him. "Come

on, Lor. Let's grab Rose and hit the road. Sooner we get back, the better."

Laura was stunned. Things had gone from sweet to sour in a matter of minutes. Everyone had been having fun, enjoying each other's company, and now it was suddenly over. "Are you winding us up, Dan? You never have work on a Sunday."

He gave her a subtle glare. "I know, and I'm really pissed off about it, but it's an emergency. I can't risk my job by saying no, can I? I've only been there six months and business is slow."

"You should go," said Laura's dad, now sitting back down. He fiddled with the cards he had laid to win, whipping them back and forth against the side of his hand. "Work comes first. We'll see you again soon, I'm sure."

"Yeah," said Danny, again barely acknowledging him. "Come on, Lor. We need to leave."

"But... But..."

He put a hand on her arm, not exactly seizing her, but firmly easing her up out of her chair. She followed him into the hallway, half in a daze, and still wondering what on earth was happening. Her parents remained in the orangery, which gave her a chance to speak with Danny alone. "Dan, we can't drive home now. It's the middle of the night, and you've been drinking."

"I've had a few beers, Lor. I'm fine. This time of night the roads will be empty. We can be home in a few hours."

"But Rose—"

"Rose will sleep in the car. She won't even know any different."

"She'll be upset that we're leaving early. She and Dad were going to feed the chickens in the morning."

Danny shook his head and laughed to himself. "Chickens. Was he planning to take her on a fox hunt afterwards? Upper-class twat."

Upper-class? My dad started out as a butcher working with his uncle. What is Danny talking about? I swear, he makes up his own reality.

"Danny, please, just calm down. If this is about Peter—"

He gave her a small shove, knocking her back a step and causing her to gasp. "Don't tell me to calm down. Your dad might not have to work for a living, but I do. If I don't go in tomorrow morning, I'll lose my job. Then where will we be?"

"Dan, I don't... I don't believe you. This is upsetting me. I don't want to leave."

He grabbed his jacket from the cloakroom inside the porch and shouldered it on. "Stay here if you want. See what happens."

"What do you mean?"

"If you don't come with me now, Lor, I'll change the locks and you can just stay here with Mummy and Daddy permanently. Hey, maybe you can get back in touch with Peter. He's obviously the love of your life."

"What? Dan, I don't understand what you're—"

He turned the key in the front door. "I'm going to warm up the car. Go get Rose and our stuff. Or don't. Your choice. But make sure you think carefully, because you won't get a second chance."

"Dan..." She didn't finish another sentence because he stormed out of the house and climbed inside their car. For a couple of minutes, she just stood there in stunned silence, until her mother eventually came up behind her and placed a hand on her arm, startling her. "Are you okay, love?"

"What? Oh, yeah. Dan just has work. I can't believe it. His boss is a bit of a bully."

Her mum nodded and gave her a pitying smile. She had turned grey since Laura had last seen her, and obviously no longer went to the effort of dying her hair. "You best go then, I suppose, sweetheart. You need to put your family first."

"You don't want me to stay?"

"Of course I do, but you have a life to lead. Don't cause yourself problems on my behalf. I'll be okay."

Laura looked over her mother's shoulder at her father sitting in the orangery. He was sipping the last of his latest whiskey. "What about Dad?"

"He'll understand. Work always came first for him, too, don't you remember? Our entire life used to revolve around fitted kitchens and electric ovens."

Laura chuckled, picturing the garage of their old house stuffed full of cabinet doors and twelve kinds of handles. Her father had started a kitchen company from nothing, but the early days had been rough. Sometimes, days had gone by without Laura seeing her father, and it wasn't until he sold the company to a large chain for a hefty sum, allowing him to retire, that he spent any time at home at all. She had been going on thirteen by that point.

Just tell her, thought Laura. *Tell her how unhappy you are. Tell her Danny is beginning to scare you. Let her know you need a hug and somewhere for you and Rose to stay.*

Ask her to be your mum.

"Mum, I—"

Her dad stepped out into the hallway. "Everything okay, girls? Are you still leaving, Lori-Loo?"

Laura studied her dad and saw unkindness in his eyes. This was a game to him, but was it a contest between him and Danny, or her dad and her? What outcome did he seek?

Does he even care what happens to me? Has he ever cared?

Whatever his faults, Danny loves me, and he's on my side. He tries so hard to be a good man.

"Everything's fine, Dad. Danny's just upset that we have to leave. I'm going to wake up Rose. Then we'll hit the road. We'll visit again soon, I promise. Thanks for having us."

Her dad smiled and folded his arms. "It's been a pleasure. Rose is a little angel. Tell her we'll feed the chickens next time."

"Will do." Laura turned towards the stairs, wanting to throw up. She had made a decision, yet at the same time, she felt completely powerless.

Ten minutes later, she and Rose were belted up inside the car, with Danny behind the wheel. He switched on the engine and stared silently down the driveway before shifting into gear. Laura's parents waved them off from the front porch, which caused Rose to cry, but Danny didn't wait around.

Laura held back tears. *This isn't fair. Why is this happening?*

Danny pulled onto the main road, glaring ahead. His hands gripped the steering wheel tightly. His jaw flexed as he ground his teeth. She had rarely seen him so angry.

Danny loves me. He would never hurt me.

He would never hurt me.

I'm afraid.

Chapter Seventeen

The stairs creaked like an old lady's back. Not that the noise mattered. Danny was right behind her, stumbling clumsily upwards. A resounding crack from the sitting room below suggested that the other dead were inside, too.

"In here," said Mitch, pointing to a door at the front of the landing. "It's the only room with a lock."

Laura hurried past him, Rose in her arms, and entered the room. It was a carpeted bathroom, unexpectedly large. She placed Rose down on the carpet and ushered her to the rear of the room, where there was a cream-coloured toilet and another door that must have led into a bedroom.

Mitch locked the landing door by turning a knob attached to a brass door handle. He then grabbed an overflowing laundry basket and placed it up against the door. Seconds later, Danny started banging on the other side. It wouldn't hold for long. Laura could already hear it splintering.

She sat down on the edge of a long bathtub. It was cast-iron and painted the same old-fashioned cream as the toilet. Despite the bathtub's obvious age, it appeared luxurious compared to the cramped acrylic baths Laura was used to. The carpet beneath her feet was plush, but worn in several places. The windows, instead of being frosted, were ordinary leaded panes framed with wood. It was odd to see outside from a bathroom, but it allowed her to see that the black sky had turned a deep shade of blue. It was 5am.

How long before the police arrived? Was there any way of helping Danny? Or was it too late? Maybe it had been too late from the beginning.

That bite mark on his wrist had made him sick.

Mitch leant over the laundry basket and pressed both hands against the door. "I've seen some things in my life, but this takes the biscuit. Are you both all right?"

"Yes," said Laura. "Or no. I'm not sure. I'm alive, so I'll take it."

Rose was leaning against Laura's leg, but she reached out and touched the bathtub with her tiny hand. "Want a bath."

Laura broke out in laughter. Rose loved her baths, playing with her ducks and her foam tile stickers, and hearing her ask to have a soak was like music. She was still a child, wanting to have fun. Maybe this wouldn't break her after all.

Although she's going have to deal with no longer having a father. How can I raise her alone?

The same way you've already been doing. Danny might have paid the bills, but what else has he been good for?

The cruel voice in her head shocked Laura, yet she didn't dismiss it. Tonight's events had brought out her anger – a part of herself that she had always tried to suppress, because Danny had convinced her she was volatile – but the truth was, it felt good to be pissed off. It felt honest. Truthful. Free.

"My husband is a bastard," she said, unable to stop herself from swearing in front of Rose. "Not a wicked man, just a bastard."

Mitch looked back at her and frowned. "He's clearly not himself. We'll get him the help he needs."

As if to agree, Danny moaned on the other side of the door. It was bizarre to hear his voice. So braindead and animalistic, yet still, somehow, his.

Laura shook her head and chuckled ruefully. "I've spent years trying to give him what he needs, but he's always been broken. From the very first day I met him, I've been trying to fix him, but the only person who ever could have was him. But instead of taking responsibility for his own actions, he preferred to blame his behaviour on other people. I spent our entire marriage being the bad guy, unappreciative of his love, always guilty of aggravating him, but it was bullshit. I was never the bad guy. It was never me who was controlling, cruel, and selfish. I loved Danny with all my heart, and I tried to make him happy, but rather than be thankful, he chipped away at me every single day. Just a little piece at a time – a slice here, a chunk there – until there was nothing left of me. He made me feel like a child, confused and afraid, and he took away my chance to be an adult. I went straight from being a kid to being his possession. I don't know who I am – no idea – but you know what?"

Mitch stared at her blankly, the door rattling behind him. "What?"

She covered Rose's ears. "I want to fucking find out."

Mitch stared at her like she was mad. Monsters stalked his home, wanting to eat them, but here she was, having an epiphany about her marriage – about her entire existence.

Somehow, though, he laughed. "He's one of *them*, is he? I know the kind. My daughter was engaged to a bully. Used to tell her how to dress and who she could see. I never did like the man, but until she left him, I never understood how badly he had treated her. The night she spilled her guts to me about it all, about the control and the jealousy and the abuse – I almost went to kill him. Thankfully, my sweet Margaret calmed me down, and it was for the best. One of our proudest moments was watching our daughter walk away from that lowlife with her head held high. It took strength, and a lot of sacrifice, but she did it. Nowadays, she's married to an accountant who worships the ground she walks on. Never been happier."

Laura started to cry, shuddering as she failed to keep in her emotions. She cuddled Rose – a support blanket, and the only thing in her life that made her feel safe or brought her any joy. The only good thing about ever having met Danny. Mitch smiled at her, an expression brimming with compassion. He seemed to forget the banging at the door and the moaning from the landing.

"Mistakes belong in the past, young lady," he said. "Every tomorrow is a blank slate and a chance to start again, so don't cheat yourself by believing that you're stuck."

"I feel stuck."

"But you're not. People always think they have to stick with the life they chose, but that's nonsense. A life is long, and it happens in chapters. My Margaret and I didn't buy this farm until we were in our mid-thirties. Before that, we felt trapped in a life of barely getting by and working jobs we hated. We dreamed of having our own farm filled with our own animals, but we always convinced ourselves we were being silly. Then, one day, after an awful day at work, Margaret came straight out and asked me: Why not? What the hell was stopping us? Why does a dream have to remain a dream? Well, my Margaret might have passed on seven years ago now, but we had the most amazing life here together on this little patch of land. If you need proof that life can end up in a much different place than it started, I'm it. If your husband was a bastard, just make damn sure that the next one isn't."

Laura huffed. "Or maybe there doesn't even have to be a next one."

"Perhaps, but don't close the door on love just because you gave it to the wrong person."

There was a brief silence. Rose was on her knees, playing with shampoo bottles as if they were people, chatting to each other quietly. With no one speaking, the moans from outside soon took over, and it prompted Laura to speak again. "You don't farm any more then?"

"Nope. Retired ten years ago. Wish I'd done it sooner and had more time with my Margaret. Still, no point regretting what's already done."

Laura frowned. "But you still have animals here. I heard cows mooing."

"Oh, yes. I still have cows, pigs, chickens. I keep them around for company and something to do. Maybe it's my penance for all the meat I sold. The animals on this farm are going to grow old peacefully with me. They live better than most people."

"That's sweet. You hear that, Rose? Mitch has lots of animals here that are his friends."

She turned away from the shampoo bottles and looked up at Mitch. "Do you have monkeys?"

"Ha! I'm afraid I don't, little'un, but I promise you can come back soon to feed my favourite cow, Jupiter."

"Jupiter?"

"Yep. She's a Hereford, bigger than you've ever seen. Named her Jupiter because it's the biggest planet."

Rose giggled, but Laura wasn't sure if she understood what a planet was. Perhaps if she had spent more time at nursery this last year, she would have.

The door cracked as the upper hinge broke loose from the frame. The whole panel tilted inwards and Danny's moans from the landing got louder. Mitch stumbled backwards, almost losing his slippers, then moved towards the middle of the bathroom. "It won't hold," he said. "We need to move from here."

"Where?"

"The door into the bedroom. Come on."

Laura realised he meant the other door on the wall opposite the toilet. It had an old metal latch, which jammed a little when she lifted it, but then she pushed the door open to reveal a bedroom. Mitch pressed her forward, moving her and Rose inside. An unmade double bed took up the centre of the room, and a large family portrait hung on the wall opposite. In it, a much younger Mitch stood with a portly brunette and an attractive teenaged girl. His family. Suddenly, the farmhouse felt less homely and more lonely. This poor old man lived alone with memories of a full house.

Mitch closed the door between the bedroom and bathroom, but there was no way of locking it, and it opened into the bathroom, so there would be no way of barring it either. Laura heard the other door splintering, and the laundry basket fall over with a thud. Danny moaned victoriously, and other moans replied, more dead on the landing.

Mitch went to the bedroom window and peered outside. "Where the hell are the police? They said ten minutes." Then he went over to a large, heavy-looking wardrobe and grabbed something from inside. He tossed it to Laura. "Here. It was my Margaret's."

Laura caught the thick jumper and pulled it on. "Thanks. We have to get out of this house. They're going to pen us in."

"You're right. I'll try to hold them off in the bathroom while you take Rose and go back downstairs. I'll catch up to you and then we can get the hell out of here."

"D-Do you have a car?"

"Of course I do. Old Land Rover parked around back. The keys are on a hook beside the front door. Grab them and I'll meet you outside. If the police don't turn up, we'll get out of here by ourselves."

The door to the bedroom rattled as Danny hit against it. The old catch on the other side kept it from closing securely, and a dead hand squeezed through the gap between the door and frame. Quickly, the gap grew wider, and Conner's pasty, expressionless face appeared. A patch of his forehead was missing, glistening with congealed blood. Behind him stood his friend and Danny. Three dead young men. Three lives lost.

Someone needs to pay for this?

Who does the fish circle represent?

Mitch moved quickly for his age, grabbing a nearby chest of drawers and frantically shoving it in front of the opening doorway. It blocked off the dead and caused them to slump forward over the scratched wooden surface. Conner reached out to grab Mitch, but he stepped out of reach. "Run," he yelled at Laura, "while I distract them."

She nodded but didn't move. "Promise me you'll meet me outside, Mitch."

"I promise, girl. We're getting out of this together." He

turned back to the dead, cursing in disbelief at the state of them. "Now go!"

Laura gathered up Rose and hurried out of the bedroom's other door. She found herself back on the landing. The way to the staircase was clear. The three dead men moaned inside the bathroom as Mitch heckled them, using language she would not have expected from someone his age.

Laura redoubled her grip on Rose, who was completely silent, and made a dash for freedom. As soon as she passed the open doorway to the bathroom, a hand snatched out and grabbed the neck of her jumper, almost decapitating her. She managed to stop and catch her balance, but she failed to break free of the grasping fingers. Danny glared at her, with nothing left of his beautiful blue eyes. His spirit had left him. He was gone.

"Let go of me," yelled Laura. "Get your goddamn hands off me."

Danny leant forward, mouth open, trying to sink his teeth into her flesh.

"I won't let you hurt me any more, you bastard." She couldn't fight back with Rose in her arms, so she did the only thing she could. She leapt backwards towards the stairs. Refusing to let go of her jumper, Danny went with her. His feet twisted awkwardly and he tumbled out of the bathroom.

"Let go of me!" Laura threw herself backwards again, but this time her right foot came down on empty air. Then, suddenly, she was falling.

Chapter Eighteen

"A man's place is at work, making a living," said her dad in the kitchen, arguing with her mother. Neither of them knew an eight-year-old Laura was listening from behind the door. "Do you not appreciate anything I do for you, Lyndsey?"

"Of course I do." Laura's mother sounded like she was crying. "I love you, Keith. That's why I want you to spend more time at home with us. Laura misses you so much. Sometimes she doesn't see you for days."

"So what? She has a roof over her head, doesn't she? The girl wants for nothing, and with the way things are going, it won't be long before we're millionaires. Do you not want that?"

"No. No, Keith, I don't. Not if it means you being gone all the time, and you acting like..."

"Like what, Lyndsey? Say it what's on your mind."

"Acting like this. You never used to be like this. We were happy."

Laura's dad grunted, and there was a clink as though he were putting down an empty glass. "Oh, we were happy, were we? Living in a two-bed maisonette with no heating and a leaking roof? Just look at this place, will you? Look at what I've given you. Most women would be grateful."

"I don't care about most women, Keith. I didn't marry you to stay at home all the time, waiting to see if you even make it back for dinner."

"I earn the money. I'm the one who works his fingers to the bone, so I expect you to look after the house and my daughter."

"Your daughter? You barely know Laura. If she had been a boy, you might take an interest, but instead you practically ignore her."

"At least a boy would get on with things, instead of getting emotional. A woman's place is in the home, so stop complaining about your lot and do what I tell you."

"I should divorce you."

Laura gasped at the sound of a mighty slap. Her mother squealed, but she cut it off sharply with a deep intake of air. A moment of silence followed, and then the sound of hurried footsteps on the kitchen tiles. "Laura? Laura, is that you?"

The door opened and her mother appeared with a bloody lip. Despite her injury, and the tears in her eyes, she smiled as she picked up Laura and hugged her. "Let's get you back to bed, honey. It's late."

"Mummy, you're upset. Did Daddy hurt you?"

From the kitchen, her father grumbled. "You should be in bed, Lori-Loo. Don't make me spank you. Get to sleep, do you hear me? School in the morning. Love you."

"Love you, too, Daddy." Laura's little heart was beating fast, but she could feel her mummy's heart beating even faster as they hurried up the stairs. She quickly clambered back into bed and pulled up the My Little Pony sheets, right up beneath her chin. Her mum sat down on the edge of the mattress and stroked her hair.

"You have sweet dreams, my little Laura, okay? Mummy loves you. Daddy too."

"Why is Daddy mad at you?"

"He's not mad. He's just tired because he works so hard to give us all the things that we need. Don't you worry about anything, okay? Mummy and Daddy are fine. Just a little argument, that's all."

"You said you wanted a divorce. Like Mandy's parents."

"I was being silly, honey." She reached over and grabbed Laura's stuffed doggy and put it under the covers next to her. "Sometimes my temper runs away with me. You take after me in that regard, Laura. You say silly things too, sometimes, don't you? When you're angry?"

Laura nodded. She had got in trouble at school today for speaking out in class. The teacher had told her that she had a bad temper.

"Go to sleep now, sweetheart."

Laura nodded and closed her eyes, but her entire body was trembling. When she heard the light switch off, she whimpered. "Mummy? I don't like it when you're sad."

"Me neither, sweetheart, but that's just part of being an adult. One day you'll be married too. Then you'll understand."

"Being married means being sad?"

"Sometimes."

"Daddy hit you."

"Don't be silly. Daddy looks after us. I love you, Laura. Never forget that."

"I love you too, Mummy."

. . .

Laura opened her eyes at the bottom of the staircase. The back of her head throbbed and a high-pitched wind whipped back and forth inside her skull that eventually revealed itself to be Rose's screams. "R-Rose? Honey, are you okay?"

She kept on screaming.

Laura blinked and tried to keep her vision still. She was flat on her back and vaguely recalled tumbling backwards. Falling down.

The stairs. I went down them on my back.

Her head and shoulders had crashed hard at the bottom of her fall, and Rose's weight against her chest had made the impact even worse. As she lay there now, Laura wasn't even sure if she could move. She could feel the cold, hard tiles through her jumper, which was a good sign, but that was all.

Did I protect Rose from the fall? Is she okay?

She tried to move, moaning in agony as she placed her left hand down on the floor. Her ring finger had snapped, curving sideways like a banana. Blood tinged her wedding ring where it had dug into her skin. The pain was like lightning in her veins. Rose sat beside her, crying, but not clutching at herself as if she were hurt. With any luck, it was nothing except shock.

She's okay. I took the fall myself.

I'm lucky I didn't break my neck.

We have to get out of here.

Laura could hear the dead shuffling upstairs, but she didn't know if Mitch was okay. All she could do was get herself outside and hope that the kind old man joined her.

"Come on, baby-girl, let's get out of"—she winced—"here." It was agony getting to her feet, but she somehow made it, wobbling back and forth until she found her balance. Her vision faded in and out, and she reached blindly for Rose's hand. It confused her when Rose pulled away.

"Daddy!" It sounded like a warning.

Laura stumbled and fell back to the ground as Danny tackled her from the side. The back of her head hit the tiles and nausea overwhelmed her. Driven by pure instinct, she slid herself away on her heels, backstroking across the tiles and onto the bloodstained rug. Danny crawled after her, his groping hands snatching at her knees, his drooling mouth chomping excitedly at the air. There was no way she could get out from beneath him fast enough to avoid being bitten, so she searched for something to defend herself with. Reaching towards a small side table next to the sitting room's armchair, she grabbed the first thing her fingers touched, which turned out to be a newspaper. She groaned at such an ineffective weapon, but it was all she had, so she thrust it at Danny's face just as he lunged. The newspaper put a barrier between his teeth and her flesh, and she smothered his face with the pages, keeping him blind and unable to bite. At the same time, she reached back to the side table again with her free hand, hoping to grab something more useful. This time, she found a sturdy metal pen with a gold-capped lid. On its side was an engraving: *Itchy*. Laura's broken finger cried out as she held the pen, but it felt good in her hand. She put the lid between her teeth and bit it off.

The back pages of the newspaper had spread out around Danny's face and were full of completed crosswords. Laura had a sudden, clear image of Mitch spending his lonely nights filling them in.

Itchy. His wife must have called him Itchy.

She smiled, even as she let the newspaper drop to reveal Danny's snarling face. "You had two awesome ladies who loved you," she said, "but you blew it. It's time I signed my divorce, you abusive, gaslighting bastard." She plunged the metal pen deep into Danny's eye, feeling only a split second of resistance before the orb popped and gave way. Danny gave no impression that it hurt, even as the nib sunk halfway to his brain. The attack did, however, disorientate him long enough for Laura to crawl out from beneath him and roll back onto the tiles. She scurried to her feet and searched for Rose, spotting her standing near the battered front door, looking ready to dash out into the night.

"Stay there, honey." Laura rubbed at the back of her head and felt a massive swelling. Stars invaded her vision. "Mummy's coming."

Danny launched himself forward on his stomach and grabbed Laura's leg. He tried to bite her, but she pulled away, dragging him along like a kid taking a ride. He was heavy, and she couldn't shake him off.

"Leave her alone!" Rose dashed across the room and kicked Danny in the chest. The sound of her little foot striking his ribs was pitiful, but the act itself was the most powerful thing Laura had ever witnessed. Seeing her three-year-old daughter fighting to protect her devastated Laura. And it sent her right back in time.

Why did I never stick up for my mum? Dad is no better than Danny. Worse even.

I should have done something. But I was just a kid.

So is Rose.

"Leave Mummy alone." Rose kicked at Danny again and again.

Danny let go of Laura's ankle and threw himself at Rose, trying to grab her with both hands. She squealed and ran away, bumping up against the room's old china cabinet. Seeing her daughter in danger filled Laura with that increasingly familiar rage. Weak and disorientated, she stumbled against the back of the settee and used it to propel herself towards Danny. She collided with him hard and took his attention away from their daughter.

My *daughter. Rose is* my *daughter.*

Danny snarled at Laura, but she lashed out first, shoving him in the chest and sending him crashing backwards into the china cabinet, almost crushing Rose, who leapt out of the way just in time. He then bounced off it, landing face first on the ground in a shower of glass.

"Rose is coming with me," said Laura, growling like a wildcat, "but you can keep the furniture." She placed her hand into the gap behind the hefty wooden cabinet and pushed. For a moment, she feared it was attached to the wall, but then it tipped forward and, at a certain point, took on a life of its own as gravity took over and sent it crashing down on top of Danny. Plates and glasses smashed on the tiles in a shattering cascade. It almost sounded like applause.

Laura took a step back, pulling Rose close to her.

Danny was pinned beneath the china cabinet, and he tore up his hands and arms on the broken shards as he tried to drag himself free. He wasn't going anywhere.

Laura bent over to catch her breath. The violence felt good, and she wondered if that should disturb her. She decided, no, because it wasn't truly the violence that she enjoyed. It was the power. She was taking back her life, even if she had to crush Danny to do it.

Rose stood beside Laura and took her hand. Only three years old, but she seemed to understand that her daddy was a bad man. Perhaps she had always known it. It was her and Mummy against the world now.

"I love you with all my heart, Rose."

"I don't feel very well, Mummy."

She gave her daughter a hug. "You're hungry, tired, and terrified. And it's my fault. I'm so sorry, baby-girl. Things are going to get better real soon, okay?"

Rose nodded and showed no sign of distrusting the statement.

The sound of footsteps on the staircase caught their attention, and Mitch appeared on the bottom step. "Christ!" he said, surveying the mess. "That cabinet's been in my family ninety years."

Laura groaned. "I'm really sorry, Mitch. I think I ruined your pen, too."

He looked down at Danny and saw the metal pen jutting from his eyeball. Surprisingly, he leant down to retrieve it, yanking it free with a sickening *plop*. "Nothing a bit of Fairy Liquid won't solve."

"Itchy, huh?"

He wiped the pen off on his pyjama bottoms and blushed. "Margaret's idea of a joke. Itchy Mitchy. I used to get eczema."

"That's cute. Can we go now?"

He nodded. "The others are upstairs, but I don't know for how long. Let's get to the car."

"Okay, but only if we can stop at McDonalds."

"You'll never catch me in one of those places. How about we eat at the police station?"

"Deal."

"Grab those car keys off the wall, will you? You drive?"

Laura nodded.

"Good, because my eyesight isn't that great in this light."

"No problem."

Laura grabbed the car keys and they hurried out of the door, entering the weakening darkness of a morning about to give way to dawn. Laura went to check her watch but realised it was missing. The strap must have snapped when she'd tumbled down the stairs, or perhaps Danny had yanked it free during his attack. It had a been a twenty-seventh birthday gift from him, with an inscription on the back: *Danny and Laura forever*. He could keep it. She'd buy a new one.

The air outside was cold, but Laura was sweating with exertion. The house was filled with the stench of rotting, bleeding meat, but outside she smelled manure and hay. In the barn, cows mooed, no doubt wondering what all the commotion was about.

"My car's around back," said Mitch. "Come on."

They started moving, but something in the trees at the edge of the fields caught their attention. Torches. Shafts of light bounced between the gaps of the nearby wood, lighting up the shadows.

"The police," said Laura. "They're here."

"About damn time."

A moan alerted them as a figure moved through the darkness around the low stone wall. It was the original zombie, the one with the bent-back arm. He hadn't seen them and was just wandering around aimlessly.

"They're really dead, aren't they?" said Mitch. "I didn't believe you at first – of course I didn't – but upstairs, when I saw them up close... This is Hell on Earth."

"It's not. There's a company behind all this. They have a logo. Two fish chasing each other in a circle."

"Huh, sounds like Le Grande Mer."

"What?"

He looked at her and shrugged. "Le Grande Mer. French, I think. They have a logo like you mentioned."

Laura didn't know why she was interested, at least right

now with the dead behind and in front of her, but she had a burning desire to know who was responsible for tonight's horrors. No more letting bad things happen without sticking up for herself. "What kind of company?" she asked, eyes on the bouncing torchlight coming through the woods.

"Agriculture. I used to buy pesticides and cattle feed from Le Grande Mer back in the nineties before Margaret and I took the farm organic. I remember the logo on their canisters: two fish in a circle. Makes sense – I think LGM owns two-thirds of the world's fisheries. At least they did."

Laura groaned. "I don't think we're talking about the same company. This is bigger than fish."

"Don't be so sure. You'd be surprised how long the arms of some of these worldwide conglomerates can be. Le Grande Mer was into a lot more than fisheries, even back then. I'm sure they've only grown in the decades since. Hell, Volkswagen was started by the Nazis. My father used to spit every time he saw one of their cars on the road. Companies don't have a conscience like people do."

"Some people don't have consciences," she said.

"I suppose you're right."

"Help will be here any minute," said Laura. The torches were now right at the edge of the woods. Soon, they would enter the small field leading up to the farm. She squeezed Rose tightly in her arms and breathed in the scent from the top of her head. "Thank you for helping us, Mitch. I'm sorry we dragged you into this."

He waved a hand to dismiss her. "My life needed a little excitement. I'm sorry about your husband. Maybe there'll be a way to help him."

"Maybe." It was a nice thought, and Laura didn't relish Rose being without a father, but even if some miracle brought Danny back, her marriage would still be over. It had taken the worst night of her life to open her eyes. She had survived Hell, and it had lifted the veil Danny had placed over her eyes. There was nothing bad or weak about her. She was a strong woman capable of anything. Nobody was going to hold her back. Not any more.

Rose had her head buried in Laura's neck, facing over her shoulder towards the house. She began to mumble, then she cried out. "Mummy! Bad men."

Laura half turned, taking her eyes off the tree line and glancing back towards the house. Conner and his friend were stumbling out through the front door.

"We have company," said Laura. "What do we do?"

By this time, the original dead man had spotted them and was stumbling across the yard. He would reach them long before help did. So, too, would Conner and his friend.

Mitch grabbed Laura's arm and got her moving. "The barn. You can climb up into the loft."

"You think we should hide?"

"I just think we should get our feet off the ground. Come on, let's move."

Mitch hurried towards a long metal shed about thirty metres away from the farmhouse, and Laura followed. The structure gave off a horrible stench, but it wasn't as bad as dead. All the same, Laura wrinkled her nose as she got closer and tried not to breathe too deeply.

"Stinky, Mummy."

"It's just farm smells, honey."

Mitch grabbed a large swinging door and pulled it open a few feet. Laura slipped through the gap and entered a straw-covered pathway between two rows of stalls. Cows stood on one side and pigs on the other. All made a fuss when they saw Mitch.

"They think they're getting fed," he explained amidst

the urgent mooing and the grunting pigs. "They won't be happy when they realise they're not. Come on, over here."

At the rear of the barn was a wet area full of hoses, watering cans, and various brushes. Mitch grabbed a rickety wooden ladder leant up against the wall and positioned it beneath a hole in the ceiling. Most of the roof was bare rafters and metal sheeting, but this section, at the rear, had joists and plaster boards in place to form a small storage loft.

"Watch yourself," said Mitch. "I forget what's in there."

Laura nodded and placed Rose onto the ladder, grabbing her under the armpits and hoisting her up the rungs. Then Laura followed, clambering up into a cold, damp space lit only by several small gaps in the steel roof. She immediately turned and looked back through the hatch to see if Mitch was coming up after her, but he was looking away, as if he had heard something. "Mitch? Hurry up."

"I can hear the police," he said. "You wait up there, okay? I'll go let them know we're here."

"No! Wait for them to find us."

He looked up and shook his head. "I need to warn them. They have no idea what they're dealing with."

Laura wanted to argue, but Mitch was right. If the police assumed the dead were just drunken troublemakers or commonplace criminals, they would attempt to arrest them, not knowing that a single bite might doom them to the same fate as Danny. Police officers were people, with families and children. They needed to be warned.

"Okay," said Laura. "Just be careful. The dead are right outside."

Mitch grabbed the ladder and moved it back up against the wall. Then he grabbed a pitchfork hanging from a hook, holding it in his hands like a spear and weighing it up until he seemed satisfied. "Don't come out unless you know it's safe, okay? Cover up the hatch. Last thing we need is the little'un falling out."

Laura was reluctant to block out the meagre light inside the loft, but she did as she was told, sliding a small wooden square into place and covering the hole. It left her and Rose in near darkness. Rose whimpered, but Laura was able to keep her calm by kissing her forehead and singing quietly in her ear. *Baby shark. Doo doo do-doo do-doo.*

She listened as Mitch shuffled out of the barn, once again exciting the cows and pigs, and then she dragged herself towards the roof at the rear of the loft. She attempted to see out through a gap in the steel sections, and it gave her a surprisingly good view of the farm. The sun was rising behind the trees, and birds chirped, a primal sound that seemed to speak directly to Laura's body.

Morning was here.

Chapter Nineteen

Laura saw Mitch stumbling along quickly. Conner and his friend chased after him, and over a long stretch, they would surely catch up. Luckily, the old man was heading right towards rescue.

The police had exited the woods and were now heading through the field. There wasn't yet enough light for Laura to see clearly, but the men were all dressed in dark clothing. They also seemed to be carrying equipment. Between them and Mitch, the original dead man staggered back and forth, seemingly unsure of which target to pursue. Mitch detoured to the left, in order to cut a wide path to avoid him, and once he reached the field, he called out to the police.

"I'm the one who called you," he said. "You need to listen to me. You need to be careful."

"What do you mean?" one of the police officers shouted back. He was slightly different to the others, wearing a yellow armband around his bicep. "Identify yourself."

"Mitchell Chegwin. Look, the man behind me... he's infected with something. You have to deal with him carefully. If he bites you..."

"Sir, is anybody else here? There was a car accident on the nearby road. One heck of a watercolour painting. Looks like people were hurt."

Mitch moved within twenty feet of the police and slowed down. Laura squinted to try and see more clearly, and she counted at least half a dozen men crossing the field, all wearing the same dark clothing. They formed a strict line.

Mitch slowed to a stop, and when he spoke again, he sounded unsure. "Who are you people? You don't look like police officers."

"Sir? We need to know how many of you there are in need of help. Has anyone from the car crash made it here?"

Mitch was silent. He remained still, even as Conner, his friend, and the broken-armed dead man approached from behind. "I don't know about any car accident," he said. "Someone woke me up in the middle of the night, banging at my door, and when I answered they attacked me. I slammed the door and called the police. Are you here to help?"

"Yessir, we came here to help you, but you informed the dispatcher that there were other people with you who needed help. I don't like having my feathers plucked, friend, so tell me... where are they?"

Mitch took a step backwards. He glanced back to check on his pursuers, who were close behind him now. "They're dead," he said. "I thought they were just injured when I called for help, but... but they're dead. You might not believe me, but you will soon." He turned around to face Conner and the other dead men, then started walking backwards into the field instead of towards the police officers. "Or maybe you already know what you're dealing with. You're not police, are you?"

Laura had a lump in her throat. *Why is he so nervous? If they're not police, then who are they?*

The man with the yellow armband stepped after Mitch, carrying something across his chest. "Sir? Are you sure there is no one else here?"

Mitch kept walking backwards through the field, glancing back and forth between the dead and the men dressed in black. "I'm sure. It's just me, you, and a bunch of walking dead people. You don't seem very surprised about that."

"I'm not," said the man, and he lifted something in his arms.

The world was set on fire.

Laura gasped and covered her mouth. There was no way the men in the field would hear her, but she didn't want to scare Rose. Her horror, however, was almost too much to contain.

Mitch was a human torch, having been ignited by a jet of fire leaping from the black-clad man's hands. He wheeled around frantically, arms flapping, and released the most hellish of screams. His anguish lasted mere seconds, however, as the flames ate up his vocal cords and destroyed his voice. The line of police officers marched past him, leaving him to burn to death.

No, they're not police officers. They're something else.

The van driver's people. Le Grande Mer?

Laura held Rose close and whispered in her ear. "Baby-girl, I know this is all really hard for you to understand, but I need you to listen to Mummy. I need you to listen and do exactly as I say. Do you understand?"

"Okay, Mummy."

"I need you to be quiet. You can't speak. You can't cry. You can't make any noise at all. Not until I tell you it's okay.

Promise me, Rose. I need you to be a big girl and do what I'm telling you. Promise me you won't make a sound."

"I promise, Mummy."

"Good girl. Now be quiet. Mummy is going to be quiet too. We'll be quiet together."

Rose made no sound, and Laura tried to be as silent as she could. The problem was, her breathing was panicked, and she thought she could hear her own heartbeat thudding in her chest. The cocoon of the loft felt safe, but how good a hiding spot was it, really? The ladder outside was a dead giveaway.

She looked back out through the gap in the roof, praying that no one would be able to see her as she spied. Mitch had fallen in the middle of the field, his body burning away like a tiny bonfire. The line of black-clad men advanced, not missing a single step as they lit up the broken-armed zombie in flames. The dead man didn't scream out like Mitch had; he just carried on shuffling until the weight of his own burning body became too much and sent him toppling onto his front. Like Mitch, he continued to burn long after going still.

"We need one alive," the lead man shouted to the others. "Any will do."

One of the men launched forward out of the line and fired a gun. The blast echoed off the nearby trees and sent birds into the dawn sky. A black shape arced across the field and struck Conner in the chest. He stumbled backwards and fell, suddenly enveloped by a thick net. The shooter returned to the line, just as a jet of flame spilled forward and engulfed Conner's friend.

"That looks like all of them out here," said the lead man. "I want a full check on the area. That old man was lying to us. There are survivors from the crash. A woman made a call on Osbourne's satphone. I want her found and contained."

Laura's blood turned cold. These men were involved with the van driver and his cargo. Behind everything that had happened tonight. Bad men.

Just stay hidden. They might go away.

And then what? They'll track me down. They're searching for me.

No, I lied on the phone. I said my name was Sarah.

Laura hugged Rose and shushed her. Time stood still, and it was an age before she heard anything again.

"The farmhouse has been cleared," said a voice right outside the barn. "There's only one Z inside, trapped beneath an old cabinet. You want me to extract it?"

"Negative. We have a live one, so let's torch this place and get out of here. Bravo team is dealing with the mess on the road. I want to get back to the road and help expedite things."

Laura's head spun. The men were talking about Danny like he was a specimen. They had also said something else.

They're going to burn down the farmhouse.

Just stay quiet. They don't know you're here.

"What about the female who made the first call?"

"I don't know," said the leader. "But if she makes the slightest peep about this, we'll know about it and we'll deal with her. Her days are numbered. Torch the house, maybe she's hiding inside."

"Roger that. What about the barn?"

Laura covered her mouth to keep from crying out.

No. Please.

"Torch it."

"Torch it?"

"Yes, is that a problem?"

"Well, it's full of animals, sir. Seems a little cruel to torch it. What if I clear it and find nothing? Can we not just leave it? Come on, Cox, have a heart."

The leader huffed, and Laura waited on tenterhooks for his reply. "Fine," he said. "But you check every inch of it. We can't afford to miss anything here. Crouse is already on the warpath about all this. We don't want to give him a reason to look at us."

"Roger that, sir."

Laura flinched as the barn door swung open. She peered through a tiny gap on the opposite side of the loft and saw a young blond man enter. He was little older than Conner had been, but he looked far more dangerous. He was wearing black body armour covered in pouches and equipment, like he was ready to wage war.

The sun had now fully risen, and its rays spilled down the walkway, lighting up the cows and the pigs, who once again made an excited racket.

"Hey, there," said the blond man. He was talking to one of the cows. "You see anything, girl? Anyone hiding out in here with you?"

Just me and my daughter, thought Laura. *Please don't find us.*

The blond man reached out a hand and patted the cow on the nose, and the animal seemed more than happy to accept the gesture. It had obviously been made friendly by Mitch's kindness.

What will happen to them now that's he's dead? Will they end up on somebody's dinner plate?

The man strolled down the centre of the barn, his eyes flicking left and right. His hands hovered by his side, at the ready. He was a soldier. Or maybe just a trained killer.

A killer who happens to love animals.

Laura rocked Rose gently in her arms, but rather than keep her quiet, it had the opposite effect. "Mummy, I'm cold."

Laura shushed Rose and then froze stiff. Her daughter was three years old. Three years old and far too young to focus on being quiet for minutes at a time. She had forgotten her promise, but it wasn't her fault.

But now they're going to kill us.

The man in the barn stood in its centre. Slowly, he glanced back towards the wide door, which had swung most of the way shut. Then he stared up at the loft, having clearly heard Rose's voice. He knew exactly where Laura and her daughter were hiding.

"Who's here?" he demanded. "Show yourselves, right now."

Laura was still frozen. Her hand was over Rose's mouth.

"Look, I heard you talking up there, so show yourself, or I'll light this place up and leave you to burn."

You're going to do that anyway.

I can't let him hurt Rose. I have to do something. Anything.

The man shrugged. "Okay. You had your chance. There's nothing I can do for—"

"No! Wait!" cried Laura. "Please."

The man put his hands on his hips and sighed. He didn't carry a flamethrower, but he did have a large black handgun fastened by a strap to his vest. "Come down."

Laura grabbed the hatch cover and slid it aside. She blinked as the light spilled in from below, and she held Rose tightly in her trembling arms in fear of dropping her. "Please don't hurt us."

"You need to come down. We're here to help."

"No, you're not. I've been watching you. You're here to cover this all up. You're behind the dead people out there."

Despite his young age, the blond man wore a menacing smirk, like a serpent about to strike. "Then it's clear that you know too much. Unless you want to suffer, you best come with—"

"Mummy! Mummy, I want to go home." Rose was close to tears. Every time she heard a stranger's voice, things turned bad. She was exhausted and afraid. "Please, Mummy."

The blond man's expression changed. No longer did he look dangerous. He looked devastated. Both his hands moved up to his chest, and he laced his fingers together. "You have a child with you?"

Laura peered through the hatch and nodded. She moved Rose so that she was visible. "Yes. Her name is Rose. She's only three years old. Please, don't hurt her. I'm begging you."

The man swallowed, and it was several seconds before he spoke again. He looked at Rose the whole time. "You can't say anything."

"I won't. I promise."

"No. I mean you can't ever breathe a word of this. If you make it out of here alive, you might feel like running to the papers or calling the police. Don't. They'll know about it and they'll kill you."

"Le Grande Mer."

He covered his face with a hand and sighed. When he looked at her again, he looked sick. "If you want your daughter to live, you'll forget everything. This never happened. They don't know about you, and the only way to survive is by you keeping it that way. Whatever happened to you tonight, you have to forget it and never mention it."

Laura nodded as if she understood, but it was only half true. "What do I do now?"

"You put that cover back in place and you keep on hiding. With any luck, we don't burn this barn to the ground and you can get away later when it's safe. Do not make a sound. My arse is on the line too. You're lucky I don't have it in me to kill a kid."

Laura nodded, wanting to smile and thank him, but too terrified. "Wh-What's your name?"

He shook his head and chuckled. "Agent Smith." He grunted at her. "Go on, then. Hide!"

Laura pulled the hatch cover back into place and shuffled back to the rear of the loft. She told Rose, once again, that she needed to be quiet. This time, she prayed she would be.

The young soldier marched out of the barn and shut the large swinging door. Immediately, he was questioned by his superior. "Anything inside?"

"Just cows and pigs, sir. I checked every inch of the place – sties and stalls – but there's nothing in there but shit and shovels."

"Are you positive?"

"One-hundred-per-cent. I don't want to burn a load of animals to death, so I made damn well sure. It's clear, Cox. We can leave the barn standing."

"Okay, Roger that. We're about to light the house, so stand back. Once we get the fire going, we're bugging out before the fire brigade arrive. Hopefully they'll treat this like a commonplace tragedy."

The blond man huffed. "Thatched roofs are a liability, sir. Poor old guy didn't stand a chance."

"Indeed. We're taking the other bodies with us, so go see if Barton needs help."

"Yessir."

Laura couldn't see the farmhouse from inside the loft, so all she could do was listen. She heard men talking, joking and bickering. She heard them heaving and puffing as they carried what must have been bodies and equipment. Then she heard a strange, subtle sound that eventually revealed itself to be the burning of a fire. It was like an angry wind. Glass shattered. Oxygen ignited with several loud *pops*. Mitch and Margaret's dream home was burning to the ground.

"We placed the old boy inside," said one of the voices. "Investigators will assume he burned up in the house. The rest are sacked up and ready to go."

"A-One," said the leader. Cox. "Who's got the live one?"

"Barton and Leather have it secured and ready for exfil. Transportation is already waiting."

"Good job. Let's wrap this up."

Laura felt dizzy with anxiety and a mixture of fear and hope. The scene of the crime was being destroyed, but – dare she think it – it sounded as if the men were departing. Several of the voices sounded farther away.

The stench of smoke entered the barn, and a thick black smog spread out everywhere. The cows and pigs voiced their unhappiness, but most of the smoke rose upwards into the rafters. It soon entered the loft.

Rose began to rub at her eyes and then started to clear her throat.

Laura risked speaking, sure the men outside were now far enough away that they wouldn't hear her whispering. "Don't cough, honey. Please, you have to hold it in. You have to keep quiet."

Rose managed to keep quiet for almost five minutes before breaking into a coughing fit.

But it was okay. The men had gone. Laura watched them disappear back into the trees, leaving nothing behind but a sunlit field and a blackened circle of dead grass where Mitch had burned to death. His body was now gone and it looked like nothing more than old bonfire pitch.

Laura rubbed at her stinging eyes, tears soaking her cheeks. She cleared her throat. "Come on, baby-girl. It's time to get out of here."

Laura moved the hatch lid, and then realised there was no way to fetch the ladder. The drop was a good ten feet onto concrete, but at least there were patches of muddy straw to break the fall. There was no option beside dropping and hoping for the best, so she would have to do what was necessary. If they stayed in the loft, they might eventually suffocate on the billowing smoke coming from the burning house. The heat was also becoming hard to bear, and Laura's forehead was clammy. Her fringe was soaked.

"Wait here until Mummy tells you, okay, baby-girl?"

Rose nodded, looking ready to pass out from tiredness. Usually, she might have protested at being left in the dark alone, but she was in a weary daze. Laura perched herself on the edge of the loft hatch and peered down at the concrete below. Her body cried out not to do it, and it would take a heavy dose of willpower to let herself fall.

I need to get Rose out of here.

Laura gripped the opposite edge of the hatch, leant forward, and took the plunge. She tried to hold on and hang from her arms, but the sudden weight of her dropping body was too much and she lost her grip immediately. It slowed her descent only a tiny amount. Her heels came down on the concrete, and a bolt of lightning shot up her spine. She flopped backwards, head thudding down against a pile of hardened straw. A universe of stars exploded through her vision.

I'm dead. I have to be. After all this...

Moaning in agony, Laura just lay there, not wanting to move.

"Mummy?"

Laura couldn't speak at first. "M... Mummy is okay. Wait... Wait there."

She still needed several minutes to work through the pain, and it was an utter relief when she moved all four of her limbs. Other than what would likely be a colossal set of bruises – and a probable concussion – she was okay. She fought her way back to her feet and went to retrieve the ladder. Climbing it again was an agonising ordeal, but seeing Rose's face at the top was enough of an incentive to get her up it. She carried her daughter down to safety. "We're going home now," she said. "Everything is going to be all right."

They walked down the centre of the barn, hand in hand, fighting their way through the smog. By the time they reached the swinging door, they were covered in soot.

"Cover your eyes, honey." Laura shoved the door and swung it open. The smoke billowed in, but so did fresh air. Thirty metres away, the farmhouse was a towering inferno climbing into the dawn sky. The thickest of the smoke rose upwards, and with the barn door open, the cows and pigs would now have a better chance to breathe.

"Fire," said Rose, her eyes wide and swirling with the reflected flames. "Wow."

Laura shivered, glad to be warm again, but she wished the heat source had been something else. It was almost as if she could feel Mitch and Margaret's memories going up in smoke. "Let's go, honey."

Laura reached into her pocket and plucked out Mitch's car keys. She found his old Land Rover parked around the back, just like he had said. It might be dangerous heading back to the road, but she didn't have the strength left to walk. There were fields behind the farmhouse as well as in front, stretching off for half a mile in the opposite direction to the woods. That was the direction she would take, puttering carefully through the countryside until she had no choice but to re-enter the road.

She unlocked the Land Rover and put Rose inside, sitting her on the front passenger seat. She looked so tiny there, her legs dangling in the footwell. Then Laura went and got in behind the worn steering wheel. The engine spluttered, but it came to life on the second try. Things finally felt like they might be all right.

But I have to forget this ever happened. If I try to hold them accountable, they'll kill me like they did Mitch. All that matters is protecting Rose.

And yourself, Lor. It's okay to think about yourself. In fact, it's long overdue.

She put the Land Rover in gear with a grinding *clunk* and then started across the fields, leaving behind the only man she had ever loved. And hated.

Goodbye, Danny. I hope you find some peace.

Chapter Twenty

Laura's mother opened the door, obviously surprised to see Laura standing there covered in soot, blood, and grime. Rose resembled a sickly orphan standing beside her. "L-Laura? What on earth—"

Laura pushed passed her mother and stepped into the hallway. She had parked Mitch's Land Rover at a supermarket half a mile away. The last thing she wanted was to be found in possession of a dead man's car. She also didn't want to walk alongside the road in the state she was in, but she had known a way to avoid that. The reason she had picked the supermarket as the place to leave the car was because of her childhood memories. The supermarket had been constructed when she was a kid, and she still remembered the derelict train station fenced off behind it, and the remnants of the old track. The wasteland stretched all the way from the supermarket to right near her parent's three-acre home. It allowed her to stroll unseen by those who might attempt to help a bleeding woman walking with a child at eight in the morning.

Laura looked down now and realised she had tracked mud onto her parent's carpet. Once that would have filled her with dread, but now she didn't give the smallest of fucks. "Where's Dad?" she asked her mum. Rose was clearly pleased to be back at Nanny and Grandad's, but she was too tired to break away from Laura's hip.

"In the kitchen eating breakfast. Honey, what is going on? What's happened to you?"

"A lot. I need you to go and get Dad. There's a lot I need to—"

"Lori-Loo?" Her dad entered the hallway, having obviously heard her voice. "I thought you went home? Where's Danny?"

"Danny's dead." She held Rose against her, wondering how exactly she would cope with this. "He's dead because you let him drag us out of here at midnight with six beers in his system. In fact, it's a miracle Rose and I aren't dead as well."

Her dad frowned and folded his arms. "Laura, it's not my responsibility how you live your life."

Laura sneered. She took a step forward, hands clenching into fists. She had survived the zombie attack tonight, so she was in a pretty bad fucking mood. "Did you fucking hear me? I said Danny's dead. Do you ever think about anything outside of what you want? Do you ever stop playing your pathetic little power games? Danny is dead, and it's because you did nothing to protect me and Rose. You should never have let him drag us out of here. In fact, I still can't figure out why you did."

"Now look here, Laura—"

"No, Dad. You shut your goddamn mouth and listen to me for once. I've dealt with one abusive bully tonight, and I'm more than happy to deal with another. Rose and I are going to be staying here for a while, okay? In fact, we never left here last night. Danny had one of his moods and stormed off by himself. We haven't heard from him since. Do you understand me? It's important that you're hearing everything I'm saying."

Her mother was clutching at herself nervously. "Honey, if you're in some kind of trouble..."

"You have no idea, Mum, but if you care about me and Rose at all, then you will do what I'm telling you. No one can know that we left with Danny. He was by himself when he drove away."

"If the police turn up at my door," said her dad, "I won't lie."

"You will lie, because if you don't I'll make you pay."

He stepped up to her, pointing his finger in her face. "Don't you threaten—"

She batted his finger away and shoved him in the chest. The shock on his face was divine, and she breathed it in like *Chanel No. 5*. "You're done throwing your weight around, Dad. The women are in charge now. Either you get out of our way, or I'll find the best solicitor in town and have Mum divorce you."

"She would never do that!"

"Are you sure?" She turned and looked at her mum. "I'm sorry I never stood up for you when I was younger, but I'm here now. You're not alone. If you say the word, we'll get the ball rolling. This time next year you can have half of everything Dad owns. More. He'll be lucky to keep his shirt."

Her dad laughed, as if he could barely believe his ears. "I'd love to see you try."

Laura turned to him, a vicious smile on her face. "I love you, Dad, but I remember every black eye, every bust lip, and every bruised wrist you gave Mum. I'll happily remember it all before a judge. Hell, I might even make up a few details just to make it worse for you. Your pals at the Rotary Club would love knowing they have a woman beater in their ranks. Pretty sure your dinner party invites would dry up pretty quickly. And what's a life without golf buddies, huh?"

"Laura, how dare you. I gave you everything in life and this is what you've amounted to?"

"You gave me nothing! You stripped me of any hopes and dreams I ever had for myself. You taught me that a woman's role is to help a man live the life *he* wants. Then you left me in the clutches of a man exactly the same as you."

"You chose to marry Danny."

"I did choose, but if you had given me any kind of support, I could have chosen to leave him a long time ago. If you had empowered me instead of belittling me, I might have found my strength sooner. But now I have it, and no man will ever take it away from me again. Rose and I are staying here, and you and Mum are going to give us an alibi for last night. Then you'll stay the fuck out of my way, or I'll dedicate my life to bringing you down to the level you put me and Mum on. I'll take your money, your reputation, and your family. You'll spend your final years alone inside a house half the size of this one, without a friend in the world. If you don't believe me, then roll the dice. I'm young. I've got the energy for a long, bloody fight. Do you? See if I'm bluffing."

Her father suddenly seemed very old. His shoulders drooped and, standing there in his pyjamas and slippers, he struck a pathetic, weak figure. She knew that his only desire at this point was to have an easy life, which was why she had threatened his peace.

"I think you've lost your mind, Laura, but I take no issue with you and Rose staying here. Danny is really... dead? Truly?"

She nodded. "I haven't even begun to process it yet, but Rose is going to need family around to support her. That isn't going to happen if the police know that she and I left with Danny last night. They'll take her away. Danny's family will get her and probably never let us see her again."

That aggravated her father. It was obvious from the crack in his expression. Regardless of how he felt about Laura and her mother, he was very fond of Rose. "That is not going to happen. Rose is my only grandchild. No one will keep her from me."

"Good. Then we all understand what needs to happen."

Her mother looked at her, the concern on her face almost enough to bring tears to Laura's eyes, but her tears had all been shed. "Tell us what's gone on tonight, honey. It looks like you've been through hell."

"You wouldn't believe it, but after Rose and I have eaten and got some sleep, I'll tell you as much as I can. It's going to be a rough few days, but after that, things will be okay, Mum. You just have to trust me."

"I do trust you. I love you and Rose so much."

Laura looked at her dad. "Thanks for having us."

He looked away, almost as if he didn't dare make eye contact. It turned out that all you needed to do to beat a bully was call them out. Shout about their crimes as loud as you could, and they cowered like frightened little children. "You're welcome," he said with a gesture. "It's good to have you both here, whatever you may think of me."

Laura patted Rose on the back. "Okay, sweetheart. Go

have something to eat and then we'll have a nice sleep. Go on. Go with Nanny."

Rose took Nanny's hand and led her off into the kitchen. She was so tired that she barely lifted her feet as she walked. In fact, she shuffled like a zombie.

Still standing in the hallway, Laura's father stepped up beside her. "You want to tell me what trouble you're in?"

"Why? So you can throw me to the wolves?"

"Of course not. I want to help. You're my daughter."

She chuckled. "My problems are your problems, right? Hey, can I ask you something?"

He shrugged and rolled his eyes. "Sure."

"Have you ever loved me? Did you ever give two shits about me?"

"Of course I love you, you daft girl. I'm your father."

She nodded, mulling it over. "Then why did you let Danny treat me the way he did?"

"I didn't know he was like that."

"Yes, you did. You saw that I was afraid of him. His anger issues weren't exactly hidden."

He shook his head and exhaled through his nostrils. "You've got me all wrong, Lori-Loo."

"Then tell me. Tell me why you let Danny drag me away last night?"

"Because I know Danny," he said. "I know who Danny is and how his mind works. A whole year went by without seeing you. If I had challenged him, I might never have seen you and Rose again. He would have kept you from us. He's a bully. That's what bullies do."

"You kept quiet because you thought Danny would ban us from coming here?"

He nodded.

Laura rubbed at her forehead and groaned. "You're right. He would have."

"Like I said, I know him."

"Because you're a bully as well. Takes one to know one, right?"

He looked away. "Perhaps. Maybe I need to take a look at myself. I haven't been the best husband... the best father. We'll see what tomorrow brings. Anyway, I'm going to finish my breakfast with my granddaughter, if that's okay?"

"Sure. She'd like that. Hey, one last thing..."

He scratched at his ear. "Yes?"

"If you were so worried about Danny keeping us from you, then why did you humiliate him at poker?"

"Because I couldn't help myself. I might not have wanted to challenge him directly, but he was still making you unhappy. I wanted to bring him down a peg. Despite what you think, I do love you."

She nodded, then reached forward and gave her dad a hug—perhaps the first they'd had in a decade. It was a surprise when he hugged her back tightly, and when they broke apart, he appeared emotional. She wasn't much interested in that. "Love is great, Dad, but it's also a weapon. You used it to hurt Mum. It stops now, do you hear me? Maybe, if you try hard enough, you can spend your last ten–twenty years being a decent husband and grandfather."

"What about a decent father?"

"That might be a bridge a little too far."

He studied her for a moment, finally making full eye contact. "You've changed."

"I have changed, and it gives me hope."

"Hope for what?"

"That you can change too. Now let's go sit down. I'm knackered and I need a cup of tea."

"I'll put the kettle on," he said.

She nodded and moved out of the hallway. "Get used to it."

When she entered the kitchen and saw her mum and Rose smiling, she couldn't help but do the same thing. Mitch had been right about one thing: life was made up of chapters. And this... this was a new one.

Chapter Twenty-One

"Ah, a heron," said John, pulling down his binoculars and pointing through the gap in the bird hide.

His dear wife, Emily, grinned. Her spectacles were wonky, but she hadn't seemed to have noticed. "Been a while since we saw one of those. They're still my favourite."

"Tell that to Tom down the road. He can't keep his fish pond stocked because of the one that keeps visiting his garden. I had to talk him out of shooting it on Tuesday with his air rifle."

Emily hissed through the gap in her middle teeth. "Birds have a right to this world just as much as we do. If he ever does anything to hurt that heron, I'll string him up."

John patted her on the back, his old, weathered palms catching slightly on the frayed strands of her tatty woollen jumper. She must have had the thing as long as they had been married. Her lucky spotting jumper. "There, there, my dear. He would never go through with it. His temper was just up, that's all. Now, let's be quiet. I'm going to spot that red grouse today, I can feel it. Trevor posted on the boards yesterday saying it was here."

Emily rolled her eyes. "Trevor tells tales. Remember when he claimed to have seen that puffin?"

"Come on now, dear, he may well have. Puffins are spotted regularly in Cornwall. Why not here?"

Emily shook her head and smiled before lifting her binoculars and peering across the moorland. It was their favourite spot, and a regular hunting ground for many birds of prey, as well as those more gentle. In the last few years, since they had both retired from their long-term jobs as tax investigators for HMRC, they had spotted grebes, doves, woodpeckers, and grouse, alongside hawks, kestrels, and buzzards that constantly circled the sky above. It was a tiny spot abundant with life – a small patch of earth where mankind had not yet invaded. John couldn't put words to how purifying it was to be here. It removed every worry, every negative emotion. Whenever he came to this bird hide, he became insignificant. Nothing more than a spectator of life that would thrive with or without him. At this time of morning, it was like the birth of the world.

"Hmm," said Emily, binoculars pressed against her spectacles. "I think there's something moving about in the junipers over there."

John knew exactly where to look. Juniper was another rare bounty hidden in these moorlands, and only a small patch of it existed. He set his binoculars and zoomed in on the thick shrub, filled with dark fruit that could take as long as eighteen months to mature. Sure enough, something moved beneath its needle-like branches. "Is it a badger?"

"I'm not sure," said Emily, "but it's large."

"Strange time of day to see a badger. I think it's something else."

The two of them leant forward, peering into their binoculars. John's brand new set of Viking Peregrines were a lot better than Emily's old Celestrons, which was possibly why he figured out what was crawling around beneath the juniper bushes before she did. "It's... It's a person. My gosh."

He waited for Emily to reach the same conclusion, and when she did, she gasped. "Oh my. They're injured. Do you think they've been... Oh, John, it's not some poor woman, is it?"

"I don't know. We have to go and help them though."

"Of course."

John and Emily exited the bird hide through the side, hopping down the four wooden steps and coming down on the muddy path that led back to the road. Instead of taking the path, they headed off through the thicket, jogging their way through the bushes, trees, and shrubs. The moor was mostly open, with low-growing foliage, but if there had been more trees, they might not have seen the injured person.

Thank God we were here. Has somebody dumped them out here to die?

The birds they came to see scattered as they disturbed the tranquil habitat, and John found himself apologising for his transgressions. It was the only time he and Emily had ever left the hide to enter the moors, and it felt like a violation.

They stopped about ten feet from the juniper bushes, not wanting to come up on the wounded stranger too quickly. John was relieved to see that it was a man, although he wondered why that was. Perhaps because it made it less likely that this was a filthy crime committed against a woman.

"It's okay, sir," said Emily. She took off her sun hat and

placed it against her breast. "My name is Emily Anderson, and this is my husband, John. We're going to get you some help. Can you speak?"

The man moaned. He was crawling on his tummy, tangled in the lower branches of the juniper bush. One of his legs was severely broken, pointing off almost at a right angle. He wore dark blue overalls, torn and dirty. He wore one desert boot, but the other was missing. Whatever had happened to this man had been an ordeal.

"Were you struck by a car?" asked John, but the man once again replied with only a moan.

Emily turned to John. Her usually ruddy cheeks had lost their colour, and she looked ready to throw up. His dear wife had the weakest of stomachs. "He's really hurt, John. I'm going to call for help, but what should we do?"

"I'm not sure. Maybe I should try and get him out of that bush. If he keeps struggling like that, he's going to injure himself worse."

Emily nodded, so John crept over to the wounded man and knelt down. "Sir, I'm just going to gently pull you out of this bush. Then we can rest together and wait for the ambulance. Okay, easy does it..." He reached out a hand, trying to take the man by the back of his arm. John was not a strong man, but he thought he could drag the stranger along the soft grass without too much trouble.

The injured man moaned.

"It's okay," said John, continuing to reach forward. "Stay calm, sir."

The man lunged at John, seizing his outstretched hand and biting down hard. There was a split-second delay before the pain started, but then John squealed in agony and tried to pull away. The delirious man refused to let go, obviously in some kind of wounded delirium, so John yelled louder, as if it might give him strength. The sensation of his flesh ripping was surreal, and suddenly he was free and falling backwards. He landed on his rump and lifted his hand, staring at it in stunned silence. A thick chunk of meat was missing from the area between his thumb and forefinger. He could see his own blood, tendons, and yellowy fat cells.

Emily tried to gather him up, and he turned his head to the side to vomit. He had drifted slightly out of his body. All sound was an echo. All sight was a shimmering mirage.

"John! John, darling, are you okay? My God."

The delirious man broke free of the juniper bush and started crawling towards John.

"Get away!" Emily shouted. "Stay back."

John's ears popped and he returned to his body. He got a grip on himself and stood up, cradling his bleeding hand and trying to stifle his cries of pain. "W-We need to get out of here, Emily. We need to call for help. I'm hurt."

Emily nodded. The man on the ground was still trying to get at them. Delirious or not, he was seemingly intent on doing them further harm. Emily seemed to realise it, too, because she grabbed John and pulled him away. Once they got moving, panic took over and they ran. John was unsteady, his fifty-year-old legs unused to exertion, but he also felt as light as air. He reached a speed he thought resigned to his youth.

They made it back to the hide, where they had left their things. Emily pulled out her phone, but there was no signal.

"We need to... to head back to the road," said John, panting. Hot blood flowed down his arm, soaking the sleeve of his jumper and the thermals underneath.

They left their stuff in the bird hide and headed to the nearby road. Emily supported John with one hand and held her phone in the other. She lifted it into the air as if she thought it might help her get a signal. It didn't take long until she did.

She was about to dial, but someone sprang out of the trees and startled them. They had reached an area of woodland about fifty metres from the road, and John thought he could hear engines idling nearby. The man who had appeared in front of them was dressed in tactical gear, like the kind paintballers wore in their pretend skirmishes. He also wore a yellow armband. "Hey there, are you folks okay?" asked the stranger with a wide, toothy smile. "Looks like you've had your feathers plucked there, my friend. That's a lotta blood. Do you need help?"

John clutched his bleeding hand and nodded. He tried to speak, but his throat had turned dry. He gritted his teeth in pain.

"There's a man back on the moors," said Emily, still clutching her husband. "He was hurt, so we tried to help him. But... But he bit John. He bit him like a wounded animal. We need to call an ambulance. Heaven knows what happened to the man."

The stranger's eyes went wide and he nodded enthusiastically. "Of course. This needs dealing with right away. Is anyone else with you?"

"No," said Emily. "It's just my husband and me. We come here to bird wa—"

The man pulled a handgun from somewhere on his person and shot Emily right in the face.

John left his body again. The only sound he heard was a piercing tone that threatened to cut his brain in two. The only thing he saw was the indifferent expression of the man who had just executed his wife, his best friend, his soulmate.

Thirty years. Thirty years together and she's gone. Just like that.

What is happening?

John tried to understand, but his thoughts went round in a confused circle. He didn't even react when the horrible, evil man turned his handgun to point at his face. He just stared into the little black hole at the end that was still smoking from the bullet it had just fired into Emily's forehead. The only thing he managed to do was ask one tiny question. "Why?"

But the evil man didn't answer. He just pulled the trigger.

Chapter 22

One Week Later...

There was a knock at the door, which was inconvenient, seeing as Laura and Rose were halfway through popcorn and a movie. It had only been a matter of days, but already she felt at home. Rose was quiet, and jumped at every sound, but she was not unhappy. Nanny and Grandad's constant doting had helped a lot. Laura's dad had been trying his best, despite being set in his ways. A younger version of him might have been more defiant, but he was an old man now, and not as harsh or as arrogant as he had been in his youth. There was a chance he might even make amends for some of his sins, but he would likely fall far short of absolving them all. Laura's mother, too, was different. She was brighter, louder, and laughed constantly whenever Rose was around. For the first time, Laura's childhood home actually felt like a home.

Only the kindness of tomorrow can erase the sins of the past.

Laura looked towards the doorway as her mum appeared with a nervous expression on her face. "Um, the police are here, Laura," she said. "They want to talk to you again."

She sighed. "Yeah, I saw them pull up through the window. What do they want now? I've spoken to them twice already."

"I don't know, honey. You were here with me and your father when Danny drove home, so they're wasting their time by pestering you."

"Yep. Waste of time." Laura kissed Rose on the cheek and placed the bowl of popcorn into her lap. "Don't eat it all, baby-girl." She then got up and headed out into the hallway, where she found her dad arguing with a tall police officer.

"We've been through this," he barked. "Over and over. Any more and I'll be on to my solicitor. Daniel left here shortly before midnight, alone and angry. His death was no one's fault but his own."

"I understand that, sir," said the police officer. He had thick creases in the skin around his eyes and mouth, and his arms were long and spindly, like they'd been borrowed from a praying mantis. When he saw Laura, he smiled. "I'm only here to dot a few I's. We're about ready to close the case."

"Good," said Laura's dad. "See that you do."

"It's okay, Dad," said Laura. "I'll chat with him."

"Thank you, ma'am. It'll only take a minute."

"Laura. You can call me Laura." She shooed her parents away and stood in the porch to speak with the officer. "So, what do you want to ask me?"

"Nothing you haven't already been asked, I'm sure. You said Danny left here just after half eleven on the day he died. Why didn't you go with him?"

"Because I told him I wanted a divorce. He was abusive, and I was done being his victim. I'd been waiting for a safe opportunity to tell him it was over, but then Covid hit and made things even worse. When we came to visit my parents, I knew it was my only chance. Mum and Dad were here to support me and keep him from getting violent, so I did it here. Once I told him, I asked him to leave."

"Drunk? He'd been drinking, yes?"

She shrugged. "I told him to get a taxi to the nearest hotel, but he refused. It's not my fault he drove drunk."

"Perhaps. My main interest is that you were, at no time, with Danny at the time of the accident. You see, there was a report of a woman being at the scene of the crash, but she is yet to be identified. Bit of a quandary there. I've been plucking my feathers thinking who it might have been."

Laura shrugged, but inside her head was an echo. *Plucking my feathers. Plucking my feathers. This is the man who killed Mitch.* She cleared her throat and shrugged again. "Wasn't me. I was here the entire night."

The officer smiled a toothy smile. "Of course you were. When exactly did you learn of your husband's fatality?"

"Um, a few days after it happened. The police were trying to call my mobile, but I've lost it. It took them a while to track me down."

The police officer reached into his pocket and pulled out a mobile phone. "Yes, we found your phone at the side of the road. Your husband's too. Do you have any explanation for that?"

She shrugged nonchalantly, but inside she was shouting. *Shit, shit, shit.* "Danny must have taken it. He was a jealous freak. Used to steal my phone and check it all the time. When I said I wanted a divorce, he accused me of cheating, so he probably stole my phone to try and find proof."

The police officer studied her for a moment. He had deep green eyes that seemed oddly intelligent, as if he were far older than he appeared. "That makes sense. Unfortunately, jealous husbands are not all that uncommon. I'm seen my share of them in this line of work. Well, to be honest, your phone was the only new piece of evidence, so I'll leave you in peace, ma'am."

"Laura, please."

"Yes, Laura, of course. Enjoy the rest of your day. Will you be returning home soon?"

"No, I'm going to stay here with my parents. My daughter needs her family."

"Sounds like the right idea." He smiled and nodded. "Thanks for answering my questions."

"No problem." Laura went to close the door, but the police officer grabbed it and kept it from closing. "Just one more thing, Laura. I have something for you."

Her stomach sloshed, and she feared the game was up. The way this man kept looking at her...

He knows something.

"Yes? Wh-What is it?"

The officer smiled at her, but there was something dangerous behind it. He reached out and grabbed her wrist, making her gasp. Then he produced something from behind his back. "We found this at the scene of the accident. I assumed you might want it."

Laura tried to swallow, but she couldn't. In fact, she could barely take a breath. Trying not to behave like she had anything to hide, she reached out a hand and took the stuffed bunny from the officer. "This is my daughter's. She sleeps with it whenever we drive anywhere. She'll be so glad to have it back. Thank you, officer."

"Cox. It's Officer Cox. Are you sure you wouldn't like

to add anything to your story, or are you sure that you were here the entire night of your husband's accident?"

"I swear, what I have told you is the truth. I have nothing more to say. My story isn't going to change. There's nothing else to say."

The officer took a deep breath, studying her with those deep green eyes while he held it. "Okay, then," he said, breathing out. "I suggest we stick a full stop on this then. So long as your story doesn't change, there's no reason for us to meet again. Go give your daughter back her bunny." He looked her in the eyes and grinned. "Children are so precious, aren't they? We have to do whatever keeps them safe, right?"

Laura nodded. "Y-Yes. Whatever it takes. Goodbye, Officer Cox." She closed the door, unsure that she could keep it together another second longer. Once the officer climbed back inside his squad car, she slumped back against the door and let out a long sigh.

Laura's mum appeared with Rose. When she saw the rattled state of her daughter, she asked what was wrong.

"Nothing," said Laura. "It's all over with now. They won't be back." She smiled at Rose. "And guess what, baby-girl, I have something for you." She raised the bunny and shook it.

"Bunny!" Rose raced forward and grabbed the stuffed toy, hugging it against her chest. "You found him."

"Something like that, honey." She enjoyed seeing Rose reunited with her bunny, but she also knew it was a threat. A threat to keep her mouth closed or else.

Who are these people that they can turn up on my doorstep in a police car and threaten me? That they can torch an innocent man's farm to the ground and cover up a car accident involving several innocent people and a pair of goddamn zombies?

They are powerful and dangerous.

"I'm just going into the office for a minute," Laura told her mum. "I won't be long."

"Okay, honey. I'll make us some lunch."

Laura headed into the small home office that sat off the hallway and grabbed an A4 folder from one of the shelves. From inside, she pulled out a notepad and opened the cover. There were several pages already filled with her confused jottings, but she now added some more words where there was space.

* * *

Officer Cox? Mentioned at the farmhouse and also arrived in person, dressed as a police officer. Who is he?

Laura closed the notepad and sat down at her dad's computer. She opened up a search engine and her fingers hovered above the keyboard. She was done being afraid. She was done letting men threaten and control her.

Whoever you are, Cox, I'm going to find you and the people you work for.

And then, I'm going to make you all pay.

She typed in 'Le Grande Mer' and hit enter.

Her investigation had begun. She had no idea where it would take her.

ALSO BY IAIN ROB WRIGHT

Animal Kingdom
AZ of Horror
2389
Holes in the Ground (with J.A.Konrath)
Sam
ASBO
The Final Winter
The Housemates
Sea Sick, Ravage, Savage
The Picture Frame
Wings of Sorrow
The Gates, Legion, Extinction, Defiance, Resurgence, Rebirth
TAR
House Beneath the Bridge
The Peeling
Blood on the bar
Escape!
Dark Ride
12 Steps
The Room Upstairs
Soft Target, Hot Zone, End Play
The Spread: Book 1
The Spread: Book 2
The Spread: Book 3
The Spread: Book 4

Iain Rob Wright is one of the UK's most successful horror and suspense writers, with novels including the critically acclaimed, THE FINAL WINTER; the disturbing bestseller, ASBO; and the wicked screamfest, THE HOUSEMATES.

His work is currently being adapted for graphic novels, audio books, and foreign audiences. He is an active member of the Horror Writer Association and a massive animal lover.

www.iainrobwright.com
FEAR ON EVERY PAGE

For more information
www.iainrobwright.com
author@iainrobwright.com

Artwork by Carl Graves at Extended Imagery

Editing by Richard Sheehan

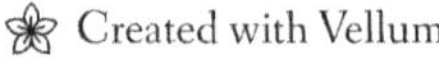